*E*linor was descending the long, winding staircase, her hand touching the rough rail. All around her was blackness, but there, out of the corner of her eye, movement.

That nasty, hunched creature, darting out of her sight. Too fleeting to make out clearly. Deeper she descended, into the chasm. They were closing in on her. If she turned, she would see them.

A light appeared, dim at first, but quite distinct. Elinor looked down at her feet and realized she had stepped off the last stair. Cool grass caressed her toes and she looked up. A door. All she had to do was turn the brass handle. Behind her, the nasty little whispering voices were growing fainter. Elinor reached forward and opened the door...

...into the most exquisite garden she had ever seen.

THE
DEVIL
INSIDE
HER

CATHERINE CAVENDISH

Dedication

To Colin, without whom…

Acknowledgments

Massive thanks to Crossroad Press for being an amazing publisher

Chapter One

*S*he was running through the woods, speeding past densely packed trees. Her breath came hard, and she couldn't feel the grass she knew was beneath her feet. She had to keep on running. If she stopped, even for a second, it would get her.

She couldn't see it. Not even out of the corner of her eye. Still she knew it was there. As always. Closing in on her. But soon she would come to a clearing. And there would be the house.

Sanctuary.

Faster she ran. Away from the unseen horror that pursued her.

Suddenly. There. A normal house, like any other, but strange and incongruous in the middle of the wood.

Bricks and mortar where there should have been timbers. Blood red roses in neat flower borders where wild flowers should have spread their leaves.

She raced up to the front door and turned the handle. Once inside, she slammed the door shut, locking and leaning against it. Outside, she could hear nothing. But it would be there. Waiting. She looked around the neat kitchen with its old-fashioned cupboards, pine table and four chairs. Surely someone lived here. But she had never seen anyone.

On the far wall was a window, hung with nets and red gingham curtains. She could go over to it and peer out. See what was out there from the safety of these four walls. She peeled herself from the door, forcing herself to walk the few paces across the pine floor. Sweat broke out on her forehead. Her hands were clammy. Heart pounding. She listened.

Silence.

"I have to do this. I have to see what's out there."

She was right by the window now. All she had to do was reach out. Pull the curtain aside and—

She woke up, bathed in sweat. *Not again.* She'd had that same dream every few nights for weeks, maybe months now. And it always ended the same way. She never saw what she was running from, but she knew it was something evil. Something so horrible that even to see it would be to look at death.

A stupid nightmare. Not real.

But it felt real.

Elinor sighed and dragged herself out of her lonely, king-size bed to the window. She pushed strands of lackluster blonde hair out of her eyes and pulled the curtain aside. Looking out, she scowled at a day that matched her mood. Rain dripped off the eaves, and trees bent under the strain of a fierce wind. November. Always a month of dark portent. Everywhere gray and sad as the leaves fell. A constant smell of decay in the air and anticipation of darker days to come.

She turned away and tried to summon up the energy to begin another struggle. If possible, she felt even more worn out than yesterday. If only she could have one day when she wasn't torturing herself.

Maybe part of the problem lay in this bedroom, which held memories…too many memories. Custom-built, light oak wardrobes and matching dressing table all acted as a reminder of better times, before her joy had ended two years ago. She had been happily married with a beautiful daughter and a good job. But on one terrible evening, her life fell apart. A drunk driver smashed into Steve's car as he drove their daughter home from a school friend's party. No one survived. Elinor's only consolation was that neither Steve nor Laura had suffered. The doctors assured her they had been killed at the moment of impact, and she clung to the hope that they had not just been trying to be kind.

She searched through her drawers for something to wear, anything that wouldn't hang off her wasted body. Listless, she dragged out a shapeless gray sweatshirt and tracksuit bottoms with a drawstring waist that she could cinch tightly. She dressed as her mind wandered back, as it did every day.

As if losing her family hadn't been enough, six months later, she'd been made redundant. She hadn't been able to find another job. Too qualified for some, not qualified enough for others. In truth, she was too shattered to handle the commitment and pressures of a new job.

She was surviving on welfare, but the debts were mounting. The house would be next to go. She couldn't carry on juggling the bills and keeping one step ahead of the bailiffs forever. The house was full of beautiful modern furniture, but no one would pay good money for it these days. Elinor had abandoned any thoughts of selling it with a certain amount of relief. At least she could keep some things around her from the happy days.

"It's as if I've been cursed by someone. Sometimes I can't think of any other explanation," she had told her best friend. "Honestly, Marnie, I've started to wonder if I wouldn't be better off out of it."

Her friend's dark eyes had flashed fear. "Don't say that, Elinor. God, don't even think it. Not for one second. Promise me. You know I'm always here for you."

Dear Marnie. She *was* always there, but that wasn't fair. She had her own life to lead. Elinor already felt she leaned on her friend too heavily. No, she must fight her own battles. God alone knew she had enough of them.

The mail arrived. Elinor poured herself a coffee, taking a deep breath before girding herself to deal with the latest batch of final demands and threats of court action. She tore open the envelope of the first one, from the bank that held the mortgage on her house. She stared at the words as they merged into one swirling maelstrom of misery.

"Payments…three months in arrears… We shall have no alternative…court action…"

Sick to her stomach, Elinor swept up the letter and the stack of unopened envelopes and wrenched open a drawer of her bureau. She threw them in to join the pile already there and slammed it shut. Out of sight.

But never out of her thoughts.

She looked at her watch. Ten past nine. The day stretched ahead of her. She opened her purse. No paper money. A few coins, and they had to last her until the welfare check hit her bank account. Fortunately, a different bank than the one that held her mortgage, or she would have had nothing but fresh air to live on. Although if those bloodsucking leeches had their way, it could still come to that.

She needed to talk and picked up her landline without thinking. No dial tone. What an idiot! It had been cut off six months ago! She rummaged in her bag for her cell. A pay-as-you-go, and she had a small amount of credit on it. Enough for a quick call anyway.

"Marnie? It's Elinor."

"Hi, El. You sound awful. Has something happened?" The friendly voice was comforting.

"Not really, I'm feeling down again, I'm afraid. I had another nightmare last night."

Marnie drew an audible breath. "Oh no. Which one?"

"The one about the house in the woods."

"Did you look through the window? Did you see it?"

Her cowardice stung her, but she said, "No, I couldn't. I couldn't bring myself to—oh, what's wrong with me, Marnie? I'm such a wimp!"

Marnie's voice came back, sharp and strong. "No you're *not*, El. For heaven's sake. It's a bad dream. An illusion your brain is conjuring up because of all the stress you've been under. You're not responsible for what happens in your dreams. How could you be?"

A wave of relief swept over Elinor. Trust Marnie to put everything back into perspective. "I'm so glad you're there. I don't know what I'd do without you. Those nightmares are so real, and they wear me down, night after night. Every time I finally get to sleep, either I'm in that house or... God, I get so wound up, I can't separate fact from fantasy sometimes."

"All I can say is that it's hardly surprising. Honestly, if they wrote a script for one of those prime-time soap operas and used the past two years of your life as a blueprint, the producers would refuse to put it on. They'd say no one would believe it."

Yet again, Marnie had got it right. Elinor sighed. "It's funny you should say that, but I've sometimes wondered whether I'm living through a lifetime of *Eastenders*."

"I'm sure it must seem like it. But you know the old saying, 'all things must pass'? It won't always be like this, El. It *will* get better. I *know* it will."

They chatted a little more and, as Elinor ended the call, she raised a silent prayer of thanks to God for creating Marnie Redman.

<hr>

That night, the wind died down to a gentle breeze ruffling the curtains of Elinor's bedroom as she finally slipped into an uneasy sleep. This time, the other nightmare assailed her.

She was descending a long and winding staircase, deeper and deeper to the depths of some chasm. She could hear chattering, whispering, but couldn't make out the words or who was speaking. Her bare, white feet took one step at a time, and she held onto a rail that snaked its way downwards. Rough to the touch.

A draft chilled her through her flimsy nightgown. The long, pale silk fluttered. Down, down she descended.

Deeper and deeper. She didn't sense walls around her, just empty, black space.

But maybe not as empty as it seemed.

Out of the corner of her eye, she caught a glimpse of something moving. The voices grew louder.

Nasty, vicious, biting little voices.

There. She almost saw it. She gasped. In a split second, she had been aware of a hideous black dwarf-like creature. But the image was too fleeting. It darted out of sight before she could fully make it out. Still she descended...

They were behind her. If she turned around, she would see them. It always happened this way. But she never turned. She always woke up.

The black cloak of dense smoke descended on her, as usual, enveloping her like a shroud. Those voices, constantly chattering and stabbing at her, indistinct but only just. If only she could make out what they were saying. She'd wake up any second. All she had to do was wait. She closed her eyes.

And nothing happened.

<hr>

"Why would anyone do such a thing?" Marnie shook her unruly black curls, folded the local newspaper and set it to one side on her kitchen table. She picked up her cup of coffee.

"Why would anyone do what?" Elinor asked, taking a sip of hers.

Marnie tapped the paper with her forefinger. "This poor man. Went out jogging early in the morning as usual and, for no apparent reason, stepped in front of a truck and got himself killed."

"Maybe he was desperate."

Marnie studied her friend's expression. She had become accustomed to Elinor's pale, drawn face and the ever-present dark circles under her eyes. Poor Elinor. These past two years would have been enough to drive anyone over the edge. But today she seemed to have a little more color in her cheeks.

Unless Marnie was imagining it. "How are you sleeping these days?" she asked.

Elinor grimaced and shook her head. "Not very well, until last night anyway. You know I've been having these recurring nightmares? Well, last night I had the one about descending down this long, winding stairway with nasty things lurking in the darkness and this smoke trying to wrap itself around me. It always ends the same way. I know I need to turn around and see what's behind me, but I never do and then I suddenly wake up. Only last night it ended differently. I'm not sure how, but when I woke up this morning, I felt as if I had actually had a proper night's sleep."

"That's good news. I always think you can cope better if you have had a decent night."

They were sitting at the scrubbed pine table in Marnie's roomy kitchen on a foggy Saturday morning. As had become the norm, Marnie was doing her best to help Elinor keep going, which was hard.

At times Marnie believed she couldn't do any more and wanted to give up. But without her, Elinor would have no one. She had no close living relatives and, with Steve and Laura gone, no family. Some so-called friends had been helpful at the start, but drifted off when things got tough.

So Marnie kept trying. She visited Elinor almost every day. Sometimes just for a few minutes, sometimes longer. During the week,

Marnie had her job as a secretary at a local private school, but as she was generally home by four thirty, she often called in to see Elinor. Frequently she would be in despair, clutching a wad of bills. At other times, she'd be in tears, hugging a photograph of Steve and Laura.

And one, never to be repeated time, she'd been clutching a bottle of sleeping pills, pleading with Marnie to let her take them. Marnie had flushed them all away while Elinor sobbed her heart out, crumpled in a heap on the bathroom floor.

"Are you all right, Marnie?" Elinor sounded concerned.

Marnie jumped. "Sorry, I was miles away. I'm fine. A bit tired, that's all. The Head wanted all the reports by yesterday afternoon, so I've been putting in a few extra hours this week. Bringing work home."

"If they need anyone else to help you out, you know where I am."

Was that actually an attempt at a smile? And the blue-gray eyes seemed more alive. Less haunted and desperate.

"You really do look better today," Marnie said.

"Do I? I do think I'm a little less zombie-like."

Marnie decided now was the time to broach the subject she had been shelving for months. "Do you feel up to going to see the bank? About the mortgage arrears, I mean. I could take a day off and come with you if you like."

Elinor winced. "I don't think so, not yet, Marnie. I know I have to face them one day but it's too hard at the moment. The letters are so vicious."

"But they'll only get worse."

Without warning, Elinor slammed her fist down on the table, spilling a startled Marnie's coffee. "Not now, Marnie. Please. I've said I'll do it, but I'm not up to it yet."

Marnie didn't need telling again. But Elinor had to do something soon. The trouble was, Marnie hadn't a clue how to persuade her to act.

———

The TV report showed a happy couple embracing. He was handsome, smiling. At thirty-one, Ian Rogers apparently had everything to live for—a recent promotion and a three-month-old son by his longtime partner.

One morning, three days earlier, he had gone jogging as he always did and never returned. The driver of the truck that hit him needed treatment for shock. He rounded the corner and saw the man step out in front of him. The driver's voice shook as he recounted his story to the reporter. It had been pitch dark and the streetlamp was out, but the jogger must have known the truck was coming. The driver said he'd never forget the expression on Rogers's face just before he hit him.

As if he wanted to die.

Marnie sighed, switched off the TV, and sank into the cushions of her comfortable brown leather settee. Suicide. From what they were saying, it had to be, but who could explain why?

Her mantle clock chimed midnight, and she decided to go to bed. As she brushed her teeth and changed into red tartan pajamas, her thoughts turned toward Elinor, wondering if she was asleep yet.

"'Night, 'night Elinor," she whispered. "Sweet dreams." Marnie lay in her comfortable double bed and pulled the duvet over her, letting her thoughts drift.

She and Elinor were the same age, thirty-five. But they had led very different lives. Marnie had been brought up in a poor neighborhood with three brothers and two sisters. Elinor Gentry had been born into money, which her father had lost through ill-advised gambling on the stock exchange. At eleven years old, she had swapped the uniform of the luxury private school for that of the local, state-run high school where she and Marnie had first met and become firm friends.

When Elinor married Steve Gentry, a partner in the firm where she'd been working as an accountant, Marnie had been her proud maid of honor. She sighed. Elinor had been radiant that day. Her long, naturally blonde hair had gleamed, and her eyes had shone with happiness as she stood side by side with Steve while the photographer clicked away.

Two years later, Laura had been born. Marnie remembered her godchild, who'd been a sunny, happy little girl with wavy blonde hair. Laura could brighten a day with her smile. Marnie's heart would lift when Laura came skipping up the drive to greet her.

As she lay there in the dark of the small, quiet bedroom, she brushed a tear away. How cruelly Elinor's world had been torn down.

But, despite everything, Marnie would get Elinor to see reason. Though she put bills aside in a special drawer, that didn't make them go away. Not really. Marnie didn't need telling again. But Elinor had to do something soon. The trouble was, Marnie hadn't a clue how to persuade her to act.

As Marnie slept, across town retired civil servant Felix Winterton was making his unsteady way home from his local bar. The dark, damp street was deserted save for a black cat who darted out of his way amid protesting meows.

Turning the corner, Felix gasped.

In front of him, a young woman was trying to battle something shadowy and indistinct. And she seemed to be losing, for it…whatever it was…slowly enveloped her. His befuddled mind tried to make sense of it. Something had her around the throat. She was trying to claw it off her, gouging deep scratches that became bloody wounds as her nails drove ever deeper.

"Stop!" he yelled.

She turned agonized eyes toward him and tried to scream, but all that came out was a muffled choking cry.

He could see it, but he couldn't believe what he was seeing. An inky, amorphous mass that kept changing shape. The young woman was tearing at her hair, jerking clumps of it out at the roots. Blood trickled down her face, and her mouth formed the words "Help me!" But that…thing…must have been gripping her too tightly for her to utter them.

He reached forward, and his hand went through it, but the contact was devastating, as if he had pierced a slimy, evil substance that sent all his nerve endings into overdrive. Despair welled up inside him and tried to suck him in. He snatched his hand away in rigid, mute horror and could only watch as the girl sank to her knees, sobbing in great, gasping chokes.

Rivulets of blood coursed down onto her white T-shirt, staining it dark in the yellow light of the streetlamp.

Her mouth opened wide again. She managed a strangled cry. "Help me!"

But Felix couldn't help her. He was frozen to the spot with fear. He watched helplessly, clasping the hand that had touched the foul smoke, as she tore at her clothes, trying to rip the thing off her. But it clung on. To his disbelief, it seemed to be trying to enter her. Through her eyes, her ears, her mouth.

Anywhere it could gain entry. Hell, some of the stuff was trying to get in through her nostrils.

She was past screaming, or trying to. Now she was trying to scratch her own eyes out.

Dear God, she was succeeding. He fainted.

Chapter Two

*E*linor *was halfway down the long staircase, her hands gripping the rough handrail. She peered down into blackness, a vast void that drew her into it. She wanted to turn and run back, but knew nothing but evil lurked up there.*

The vicious little voices snapped at her. Their breath stung her neck. Out of the corner of her eye, the vile dwarf-like creature stirred and retreated deeper into the blackness.

"Elinor."

She jumped. This hadn't happened before. The voice was a gentle whispering breeze, but familiar.

"Elinor."

The stairs still stretched before her, but the voice was getting closer. It must be waiting for her at the bottom.

The other voices stopped, as if waiting for something momentous.

"Elinor."

Her heart pounded, and her breath came in short gasps. She knew that voice. She took one step. Then another. One after the other, her bare, white feet stretched out in front of her. The staircase ended abruptly, and she was standing on cool grass.

A tall figure turned.

And she wasn't frightened anymore.

"My God! Marnie, have you seen this?" Elinor thrust the newspaper at her. Marnie piled washing into her machine.

"What?" she asked.

"A young woman was found dead in Parliament Street. That's only about a quarter of a mile from me."

"Yes. I saw it on the news this morning. They're treating it as a suicide, but it sounded pretty gruesome. Apparently some guy was with her but he isn't suspected of foul play because they found no DNA on him. She did it all to herself." She turned on the washing machine and sat at the table near her friend.

Elinor tapped the paper. "This says that the police aren't releasing all the details in case of copycat suicides, but they *do* say she tried to scratch her own eyes out. I mean, why would you do that? What could have been in her mind?"

Marnie shook her head as she picked up her coffee cup. "I dread to think. The man who was with her is being treated for shock."

Elinor shuddered, goose bumps breaking out all over her arms despite the bright Saturday morning. "It's awful to think that, while I was asleep, someone I may have passed every day on the street was killing herself in that terrible way."

"I know what you mean. And, apart from that guy, no one heard a thing."

"That's not surprising really. Parliament Street's largely demolished. I've heard they're going to build an office complex there soon, and I think the last of the residents moved out a few months ago."

Marnie's deep brown eyes studied Elinor, who asked, "What is it, Marn?"

"You're more your old self today. In fact, for the past few days, I have thought how much better you've been looking."

Elinor flicked her long hair over her shoulders, stroking the newly restored softness. "Thanks. I actually do feel much better these past few days. I think it's because I'm sleeping more regularly and when I wake up, I've got more energy."

"Ready to face the bank yet?"

Elinor took a deep breath. She had been going to tell Marnie, anyway. "I've got an appointment next Friday. You will keep your fingers crossed, won't you?"

Marnie jumped up and hugged Elinor. "Of course. Oh, that's excellent news. I'm so pleased. Now you'll be able to work something out with them. I know you will. Do you want me to come with you?"

"No, I'm OK. I think I need to do this by myself, but thank you for offering."

Marnie sat back down. "Any time."

Elinor looked at the newspaper again. "I can't get over this poor woman. Her name was Linda Crane, and she was only twenty-four. I mean, whatever could be so bad at twenty-four to want to scratch out your own eyes?"

"Maybe it's symbolic. She'd seen something terrible."

Elinor gave a little laugh. "Oh God, you're sounding like one of those horror stories you're always reading."

Marnie sipped her coffee before setting down her cup. "That's the first time I've seen you laugh in…oh, I don't know how long. You really are feeling better, aren't you?"

Marnie was right. Elinor smiled. She didn't know how or why but, from somewhere, hope was emerging.

———

Elinor was running through the wood, speeding past the densely packed trees. Soon she would come to the clearing and see the house. Sanctuary. Behind her, it was gaining ground. Coming closer. If she turned around, she would see it.

She reached the door, opened it and slammed it shut behind her, leaning against it, panting. Across the neat kitchen was the window. This time she would go over there, pull those curtains aside and face whatever was out there…

She awakened on a sunlit morning with a feeling of being able to cope. Not with everything, of course. But when she picked the mail up from the doormat, she opened every envelope, read the contents, and sat down at her polished rosewood dining table with a pad and pen, ready to make a plan.

She would get her life back on track. Elinor Gentry was beginning to find herself again after a two-year absence.

———

Three weeks later, Hazel Messinger sighed and fingered the ragged scar under her left eye. She looked back at the Sunday tabloid spread in front of her on her battered oak dining table in her overcrowded little living room. The lurid headlines screamed, "Suicide Suburb. Sixth death in three weeks!"

The report noted that a middle-aged couple, out walking their dog in the small copse that gave Hartshouse Wood its name, had been alerted when their Labrador had started barking at a clump of bushes. On investigation, the husband had found the body of a young woman, horribly mutilated, whose injuries later turned out to be self-inflicted. The couple had needed treatment for shock.

Hazel sighed and folded the paper. Standing, she wandered over to the window, dropping the tabloid in the wastebasket along the way. She looked out over the rain-soaked green fields behind her tiny, one-bedroom bungalow. Trees, devoid of leaves, gently swayed in the breeze. Such a peaceful scene. So rural. A magpie fluttered down onto her lawn. *One for sorrow, two for joy*, so the old rhyme went.

She waited, but no second bird flew in.

She raised the pentagram around her neck to her lips in a gesture she often repeated when thoughtful or concerned about anything. And what she had read in the newspaper and seen on the television news these past few weeks had made her very concerned indeed.

Ten years ago had been a time of innocence. A time before her world had been shattered. When she could hear with both ears and see with both eyes.

She turned away from the window and straightened the cushions on her worn, but comfortable, armchair. Her thoughts troubling her, she massaged her temples. She must keep busy. Tidy the whole bungalow maybe. In the hall, she paused by the mirror as she caught sight of her reflection. An overweight woman with long hair, streaked liberally with gray and wearing dark glasses glanced back at her.

How had she grown so old?

Slowly, she removed the glasses and blinked at the daylight. Her right eye was deep brown, attractive. She'd turned heads ten years ago. But the left eye was vacant, pale, sightless, and surrounded by old scars. From the day when…

Hazel mustn't think any more about that. Besides, she had far too much to do. Taking a few deep breaths, she shoved her glasses back on and turned away before striding into her untidy, cluttered bedroom, where she changed quickly into a long black skirt, black boots, and a red velvet top. People around here called her The Witch, so let them see her looking the part.

Grabbing her bag, she checked her wallet before returning to the living room to retrieve the newspaper from the bin and reread a little of the article.

"This is the latest in a series of incidents which have all occurred within a one-mile radius in the quiet suburb of Hartshouse Wood. In every case, police discovered that the mutilations present on the bodies had been self-inflicted. The injuries were all to the head and neck region. One witness, who preferred to remain anonymous, said that the woman seemed to have been trying to claw something out of her eye."

Hazel refolded the paper, her lips set in a thin line. Should she go there? Where was Hartshouse Wood anyway?

Reluctant decision made, she booted up her laptop and checked the rail enquiries website. The journey would last five hours, but she could catch the 1:15 London train and change at Birmingham and Bristol. Then she'd use the local rail service. All being well, she should arrive in the area by early evening, and she'd find a guest house or somewhere she could lay her head for a few nights.

Or however long it took.

She would need to get around. Buses would be awkward as she didn't know the area, so best to hire a car. She opened a drawer and took out her driver's license, which she briefly checked before tucking safely into her capacious shoulder bag.

She glanced up at the wall clock. 11:45. Enough time to throw some things in a suitcase and take a cab to the station.

She stopped and hesitated. Was she doing the right thing? Could she cope with this again?

Did she have a choice?

Hazel leaned back against the comfortable seat as the train glided out of the station. Oblivious to the chatter of other travelers, she remained wrapped in thoughts and remembrances, her worries enveloping her like a dark cloak.

That day in September had started like any other. She had kissed Joe goodbye, driven off to work, and gone through the usual motions of a hospital administrator's duties. Joe was on nights, so they frequently crossed the threshold going in opposite directions. But she knew when she returned home, he'd be there to give her a glass of merlot and a kiss as he left for work.

Only that evening hadn't been like all the others.

That evening, she had found Joe dead, his face a mangled mask of horror.

The coroner's inquest had brought in a verdict of suicide while the balance of his mind was disturbed. Her Joe would never have committed suicide. No, someone—or something—had killed him, but no one would listen to her.

Two weeks and three more deaths later, they still weren't listening, but by then Hazel had contacted the wife and two husbands left bereaved and incredulous.

What they'd discovered killed two of them and drove another insane.

Hazel had nearly been killed too. She would always have the scars to prove that. She had thought it gone forever, but it had returned.

And this time would be the last. Of that, there could be no doubt.

Elinor was descending the long, winding staircase, her hand touching the rough rail. All around her was blackness, but there, out of the corner of her eye, movement.

That nasty, hunched creature, darting out of her sight. Too fleeting to make out clearly. Deeper she descended, into the chasm. They were closing in on her. If she turned, she would see them.

A light appeared, dim at first, but quite distinct. Elinor looked down at her feet and realized she had stepped off the last stair. Cool grass caressed her toes and she looked up. A door. All she had to do was turn the brass handle. Behind her, the nasty little whispering voices were growing fainter. Elinor reached forward and opened the door…

…into the most exquisite garden she had ever seen.

She opened her eyes on a chilly morning and peered over at the clock. 8:00 a.m. Time to get up and start the day.

Elinor pushed back the duvet, yawned, stretched, and stood up. A few minutes later, showered and dressed, she went into her kitchen, gleaming with stainless steel appliances and granite worktops.

Another legacy from her more affluent past, when a designer kitchen with glass-fronted cabinets had been taken for granted.

Coffee in hand, she padded into the hall to pick up the mail.

Not too much today. Now she had her agreement in place with the bank, opening those official looking envelopes wasn't nearly so daunting. Today though, only junk mail. She smiled at one letter offering to lend her up to ten thousand pounds, secured by her house. "Not when you see my credit rating you won't," she muttered with a wry smile, thankful for her ravenous shredder, which also gobbled up an offer from *National Geographic Magazine*.

Seated at her dining table, she drained her coffee and booted up her laptop before checking her inbox. Empty. She proceeded to some job websites.

Elinor had started exploring them a week ago and was still tentative about them, but at least she had made a start. Not that she'd mentioned anything to Marnie yet. Best to wait until something happened, maybe before her first interview.

Elinor scrolled down through jobs she was either under or overqualified for. One caught her eye. Bookkeeper. She had qualified as a certified accountant, so she could easily do that. And she could offer them extra. OK, she might not be chartered, but she could save them money by doing more than the basics for them.

Impressed by her positive attitude, she clicked on the link for more details and was taken to a full job description, which she read carefully. The cursor hovered over Download Application. Should she? She hadn't applied for any job in two years. Was she ready?

Elinor delayed for five minutes before plucking up courage to click the mouse. The screen changed and up came the application form. Two hours later, she had answered all the required questions and pressed send.

She sat back, elation and accomplishment flooding her. Her jaw ached, her smile was so wide. Never mind the interview—the fact she had completed and submitted an application for the first time in so long was cause for celebration enough.

On a Monday evening, Marnie should be home. Somewhere, Elinor knew she had a couple of bottles of half-decent claret she had been saving. She thanked God she hadn't leaned on them for support during her darkest days. Now they'd be put to a really good use.

―――

Not only was Marnie free that evening, but she came straight over and was ecstatic. "That's great, Elinor," she said, accepting a glass of wine. "I knew you'd get there. It took a bit longer, that's all. I'll keep everything crossed for you." She clinked her glass against Elinor's. "To getting back on track!"

"I'll second that." Elinor took a deep swig. "This stuff isn't bad at all. I think I'll get some more when they give me my first month's pay."

"I'm amazed at how far you've come these past few weeks." Marnie settled comfortably into the deep, stuffed settee in Elinor's living room.

She nodded. "And the major reason is that I've been sleeping properly. Oh, I still get those recurring nightmares, but not nearly so often and they end differently. I can't remember, but did I tell you that the staircase dream ended in a doorway to a lovely garden? It was *so* real." She thought back to the dream that had filled her senses with light and hope, and closed her eyes, recapturing the warmth of the sun on her bare arms and the gentle kiss of the lightest of fragrant, summer breezes.

Elinor continued, "You know you're not supposed to be able to smell anything in dreams? I can tell you that's a complete myth. I could smell the flowers—jasmine, roses, honeysuckle, everything, as if I was awake. Bees were buzzing, butterflies were fluttering, and the sun was shining and I even heard a cuckoo. It was a perfect summer day."

Marnie sighed. "I wish I had dreams like that. None of mine ever make any sense, and I never remember them properly when I wake up."

Elinor opened her eyes. "Oh, I've often had vivid dreams. In fact, I've probably had them all my life really, but I've never had such dreadful nightmares as I have these past two years. And I'm sure that those and my lack of sleep were the major reasons I felt so unable to cope. Once that all eased off, I was able to take back control of my life."

Marnie poured herself more wine. Elinor watched her and looked up at the clock. Half past nine. "Do you want to stop over here tonight? The spare bed's all made up."

Marnie glanced at her watch. "Do you mind? I would have to leave my car here and get a taxi anyway and I'm not working tomorrow."

Elinor laughed. "That's great. It'll be like old times. We can stay up late, get drunk, and put the world to rights."

———

Three hours later, Elinor made her slightly uncertain way up to bed, following Marnie, and produced a new toothbrush for her from the bathroom cabinet. "Here you are, help yourself to anything you need. Sleep well," she said, dropping a light kiss on her cheek, which Marnie reciprocated.

Elinor waited for Marnie to finish in the bathroom before going to floss and brush her teeth. As she removed her makeup with a cleansing wipe, she studied her reflection in the mirror. Marnie was right. She did look more her old self. The deep, dark circles under her eyes had virtually vanished, even though she was quite well fortified with more than half a bottle of wine. Lack of money and social opportunities had eliminated her alcohol intake for a long time and tonight, the wine had quickly made its presence felt.

She finished brushing and rinsed her mouth with Listerine. Switching off the light, she meandered back to her bedroom, passing the spare room. All was quiet and dark. Marnie was probably already asleep. Elinor smiled.

In her room, as always, except on the coldest nights, she opened the window to let in some air before pushing back the duvet and sliding into bed, grateful for the soft pillow. Elinor had barely turned over when she fell asleep.

She was running through the wood, her hair streaming behind her, feet barely touching the ground. Behind her and getting closer… Was that breath on her neck?

Her breathing came in shorter and shorter gasps as she reached the clearing. The house. Bricks and mortar.

Incongruous. But something was different. Smoke drifted out of the chimney. Maybe someone was home today. A sudden moment of trepidation. Should she go in? She had never met the house's owners. She had even wondered if, in some way, this house belonged to her. But who had lit the fire? She knew she hadn't. Elinor hesitated. What if something bad was inside, waiting for her?

But this was her safe place. Sanctuary. Surely nothing could harm her there.

Besides, whatever was closing in behind her was much worse than anything that could be inside.

She turned the handle and opened the door. A figure stood from an armchair and turned toward her. Her eyes widened in amazement and disbelief.

"Hello, Elinor."

Chapter Three

Marnie sat up in bed. Something had woken her.

Elinor? She must check on her. Maybe one of her nightmares had caused her to cry out.

Marnie had taken off her jeans and sweater before climbing into bed and, feeling chilly, she quickly dressed and ran her hands through her unruly black hair. The hallway was quiet as she slipped silently to Elinor's room.

The door was ajar, and she sidled in, anxious not to wake her friend. A streetlamp cast an amber glow into the room, illuminating the area around the window. She could see Elinor lying on her back in bed.

But she seemed fuzzy, indistinct. What…?

A small black cloud was forming over Elinor, coming from within her. Drifting out from her eyes, ears, nose, and mouth.

Was this a dream? This couldn't be real.

As Marnie stood, transfixed, it moved. At first it seemed to be coming her way, and she backed into the hall.

The cloud drifted toward the window. She took a step closer, and it disappeared through the thin curtains.

She didn't know how long she stood there, rigid, unable to move. Trying to make sense of what she had seen while Elinor still slept peacefully.

Nothing else happened. Surely her imagination had played tricks on her. Eventually, Marnie went back to bed. But she slept no more that night.

———

The next morning, Marnie had put two slices of bread in the toaster when Elinor wandered in. She looked pale, hung over, and disheveled in a gray tracksuit at least two sizes too big for her.

"How do you feel this morning?" Marnie poured coffee for them both.

Elinor grimaced. "Nothing a couple of paracetamol won't cure. We had a few last night, didn't we?"

"Doesn't do any harm to let your hair down now and again. Especially when you've got something to celebrate." The toast popped up, and Marnie buttered the slices while she glanced at her friend's face. "Did you sleep well?" She handed Elinor a piece.

Elinor took a bite of toast. "Yes, thanks, did you?"

"Bit up and down," Marnie said, not comfortable venturing into what she had seen. Certainly not until she at least knew whether Elinor had been aware of anything.

Had she really seen a cloud of black smoke—or whatever—emanating from Elinor? Marnie shook her head. She still wasn't sure. How could she have seen that? She must stop being so fanciful. "Shall I put on the radio?" she asked. "We could catch the news."

"Why not?" Elinor said. "We'd better find out what's going on in the world."

Marnie switched on the kitchen's small TV, tucked onto a spare corner of the granite counter, then collected their cups and plates. She took them to the sink, as the news bulletin came on. She picked up a coffee cup and the dishcloth.

"Police are investigating the latest in a series of unexplained suicides in the Hartshouse Wood area near Bristol. The woman, in her late twenties, has been identified as Jessica Rigby. A witness reported seeing a strange black mass around the victim shortly before she collapsed. The police later dismissed this as a shadow created by the streetlights."

Lightheaded, Marnie staggered. A buzzing started in her head. Cup still in her hand, she turned to Elinor.

"Not another one!" Elinor exclaimed. "What's happening around here? Are they polluting the water or something? Marnie! Are you OK?"

The cup slipped out of Marnie's hand and crashed on the travertine floor.

"Good grief. You look as if you're going to faint." Elinor rushed over to her and took her arm. "Come and sit down. I'll clean that up later. God, we really must have drunk too much last night. Do you feel sick or anything?"

"What? Oh, no, no. I'll be fine in a minute. It's the shock."

"Shock? Oh, you mean the suicide. It's terrible, isn't it? I suppose the tabloids will have all the gory details tomorrow."

"Yes," Marnie replied automatically, while her mind raced. What was going on? The black cloud. The witness had reported seeing one. Yes, that *could* have been a trick of the light. That was a nice, convenient explanation, typical of the police.

Everything neat and boxed away. Another suicide for the coroner to report on.

But she knew what she had seen. That hadn't been a dream. She'd been there. She'd seen the cloud leave Elinor and exit through the window. And now a young woman was dead.

Marnie decided. "I have to go home, Elinor. I'm not feeling too good and I want to be in my own bed. Hope you don't mind?"

"No, of course not, but are you going to be safe driving yourself?"

"Yes, I'll be fine. I need to go home."

"As long as you're sure." Elinor paused. "I'll call you as soon as I hear anything about the job."

"Oh yes, please do."

From Elinor's quizzical expression, Marnie knew she wasn't putting on a convincing act, but she really couldn't concern herself with that. She needed to find out precisely where the suicide had taken place, who the young woman was and—perhaps most important of all—who the witness was and where he or she could be located.

Internet searches revealed twenty or more entries.

Most repeated the same sparse details as the news bulletin, but she hit on another one, a blog by someone calling himself "Foggy By Nature." She clicked on the hyperlink and scanned the entry.

"The police don't want me talking about this.

They think I'm a nutter anyway, so what do I care? I know what I saw, right? OK, this is how it goes. I'm out early with my dog. It's maybe five a.m. and I'm on the edge of the wood, walking on this narrow lane. There are trees on either side, and streetlamps. Up ahead, I see someone struggling with something, and I think it's a woman being attacked. What do I do?

What anyone would of course! I let my dog off the lead and race up toward her. Only my dog's a wimp. Not usually, but he is today. He's a great big Alsatian, and he stops maybe ten feet from this person and I'm getting closer and I can see. There's this young woman and no one's with her, just this black cloud, like smoke, swirling around her. My dog's whimpering like a puppy and she's trying to scream, but she can't. This thing is strangling her. At least I think it's strangling her, but maybe it's trying to get inside her, I don't know. Now I'm nearly there, and she falls to the ground and the crazy thing is that the smoke's disappeared, as if it was never there. But I know what I saw and no one's going to change my mind."

She read a dozen comments, mostly skeptical or derisory. All had been left in the past ten minutes. But Marnie didn't want to comment publicly. She clicked onto Foggy By Nature's profile. He was called David Masters and, thankfully, he'd left an email link.

Marnie wrote a brief message, telling him she was interested to learn more about the cloud because she thought she had seen it too. Would he like to meet and talk about what he'd seen? She hit send and sat back, waiting for a response and hoping it wouldn't take long.

Fear descended on her. What was she doing? She had emailed a total stranger who, by his own admission, was deemed a "nutter" by the police. More than that, she was suggesting they meet! *Best be somewhere public. Costa's or Starbucks, maybe.*

While she was still pondering the wisdom of her actions, a tuneful ping announced the arrival of an email.

David Masters. His reply was interesting. "I'm glad I'm not the only one. The police told me I must have been seeing things, but I know what I saw, and you seem to as well. A woman called Hazel has also been in touch and we're meeting at McDonald's in the High Street tomorrow at eleven. Do you want to come along?"

Before she had time to change her mind, Marnie replied. "Yes. See you there."

Marnie recognized David Masters from his thumbnail picture on the blog. Probably early twenties, dressed in a dark blue hoodie over a black T-shirt emblazoned with a werewolf. His jeans were frayed, his light-brown hair long, curly and unkempt, and he looked like the student she knew him to be from his profile. The dog wasn't tied up outside.

Probably left at home in disgrace for his earlier cowardice.

Sitting opposite David was a middle-aged woman, dressed rather like a refugee from Woodstock. Ankle-length, flowing purple skirt, black long-sleeved top and, over the back of her chair, a long thick woolen cardigan to keep out the chill. Her hands were covered in rings, Gothic rather than ornamental.

The two were engaged in earnest conversation. "Hi, I'm Marnie."

They turned and looked at her. The woman smiled and put out her hand. "I'm Hazel Messinger, my dear. It's very nice to meet you." Large, dark glasses failed to conceal fully an ugly scar that looked like a deeply gouged series of scratches, ending on her left cheek.

"I'm David." He looked serious. Almost sullen. And didn't extend his hand, but Marnie didn't expect him to. From the debris on the table, David had obviously eaten a burger and fries and was most of the way through a large Coke. The clock on the wall across from them showed two minutes after eleven, so he must have got there deliberately early. Hazel had only beaten her by a few minutes, judging by the steaming, almost full coffee she held.

"I'll go and get a coffee and be back in a minute. Can I get either of you anything?"

Both of them declined her offer politely. Marnie was served immediately. The place was nearly empty, but in a half hour or so, it would be teeming with students and office workers.

Returning to the table, cup in hand, Marnie sat between the two of them. "I am so glad I found your blog," she said to David.

"So am I," Hazel said. "Finding that made my job so much easier."

Marnie turned to her. "Sorry for being nosy, but could I ask what brings you here? I mean, have you seen this cloud too?"

Hazel burst out laughing, startling Marnie. David's expression matched Marnie's reaction.

"Oh my dear, I'm so sorry," Hazel said. "That was most inappropriate of me. I must explain. The thing is I know more about that so-called cloud than I care to. It's haunted me for the last ten years, since I first encountered it in Yorkshire. That's where I've come from to be here."

Marnie exchanged glances with David, who raised an eyebrow.

Hazel continued, "I'll tell you more later, but right now I'm interested in why you're here, Marnie. David said you had seen it too."

Marnie fiddled with the coffee stirrer with nervous fingers. Would they think she was mad? But if anyone listened in on their conversation, would they think any of them was in their right mind? She plunged in. "Last night, I was staying at my friend's house, and we'd had a few glasses of wine and went to bed quite late. I fell asleep straightaway but, very early in the morning, I woke up suddenly, convinced I had heard my friend cry out. She's had a really rough time of it these past two years and she's had these awful recurring nightmares. I thought maybe she was having another one, so I got up and went to her room. That's when I saw this… I don't know how to describe it. It was black, like a cloud or smoke but it seemed to be coming from Elinor—that's my friend. And it wasn't exactly a cloud or smoke. More a sort of amorphous mix of both. And this…whatever it was…seemed to know what it was doing." Marnie snapped the stirrer in her hand and dropped the pieces. "Oh God, I sound crazy."

Hazel put her hand over hers, her grip warm and reassuring. "My dear, you don't sound crazy at all. Not to me, and I'm sure not to David either." She looked at him. "I am right, aren't I, dear? That's what you saw as well?"

David nodded. "I call it smoke. Or a cloud. But it was both, and sort of neither. This is crazy."

"Carry on, Marnie, tell us the rest."

"There isn't much more. I thought at first it was coming for me, but it wasn't. It went out through the window."

"What time was that?" Hazel asked.

Marnie shook her head. "I didn't look at the clock. Just went back to bed and tried to sleep. I thought I must be dreaming at first, but I knew I wasn't. I mean, you know when you're dreaming, don't you?"

Hazel nodded. "David. Can you tell us where were you walking when you saw this poor woman being attacked?"

"It's called Foresters Lane."

Marnie jumped. "I know where that is. It's about a quarter of a mile from Elinor's house."

"Was anyone else around at the time?" Hazel asked.

David shook his head. "I'd been up late, playing a game on the Internet and decided to take my dog out so I could sleep later. I never saw a living soul until I went round the corner and…"

He received Hazel's comforting hand. A slight flicker of a grateful smile tugged at the corner of his mouth.

"Did you call the police, David?" Hazel asked.

He nodded. "And an ambulance. Not that she needed one. It was a bit too late for that."

Hazel glanced at Marnie and took a deep breath. "I'm sorry for asking this, but can you describe the woman? Her injuries I mean."

He seemed to shrink a little in his chair. Marnie guessed that, usually, he was a normal young man, perhaps even a bit cocky. But what he'd seen had knocked the bravado well and truly out of him.

He took a swig of Coke before speaking. "I got to her as she fell and it was like, one second the thing was all over her and then I blinked, and it had gone. Completely vanished, as if it had never been there. Her throat was clawed and bleeding and so were her ears. I think she was about to start on her eyes but…" He stopped and rubbed his own eyes. "God, I'm studying to be a vet and I've seen some bloody roadkill that looked better than her. It's like she was so desperate to get rid of this thing that she was prepared to tear herself apart."

He was shaking, and Hazel held onto his hand.

He made no attempt to pry himself away from her, as if she had become a temporary parent substitute for a boy who, right now, needed his mother.

"You're doing really well, David. There's one more thing—did you tell the police what you've told us?"

"Yes. They told me I'd seen a shadow. I think they thought I'd taken something. In fact, at one time, I thought they were going to do a drugs test. Then they seemed to change their minds and decided I was just some nutty student with an overactive imagination."

"But they saw the body. How did they explain that?"

David shrugged his shoulders. "Suicide, they said. Like the others."

"There are too many others. Surely someone is looking into this."

Marnie had been watching this exchange with mounting fear. "But if what David is saying is true—"

His eyes shot toward her, and the anger in them struck her silent. She flinched.

"It *is* true. Every word of it."

"I'm sorry, David. I wasn't doubting you for one moment. I believe you saw what you think you saw, but the significance of it is what scares the hell out of me." Marnie needed some answers. Fast. And, of the three of them seated around that table, only one seemed to have any idea what was going on.

"Hazel, please could you tell us what you know of this smoke, cloud, or whatever it is? You clearly know far more than we do."

McDonald's was filling up. Chattering students were sitting at tables close to them, too engrossed in their own noisy conversation to take any notice of what they were talking about.

After a long pause, as if she were gathering her thoughts, Hazel spoke. "Very well. What I know links it firmly to the dreams of someone nearby who is sorely troubled. Whether or not either of you believe in the supernatural, I am convinced we are dealing here with what I encountered all those years ago. It's something known as a dream demon, and this one is as powerful and evil as they come."

Marnie stared at her. "Dream demon? Is that something to do with what I saw coming out of Elinor?"

Hazel said nothing, and the dark glasses hid her expression. Fear mounted inside Marnie. "Oh no, please don't tell me Elinor's involved in all this. Please don't tell me that thing's coming from her." She looked from one to the other. David looked ill.

"I'm sorry, Marnie, but we have to face facts," Hazel said somberly. "I'm quite sure you must have suspected something or you wouldn't be here and, if I'm right, there is worse to come. You see, she has no way of controlling it. Soon it will cross into her conscious mind and possess her entirely. She has to be told what's going on before that happens, and I'm sorry, Marnie, but you're the one who will have to do this. My dear, you have to convince her that the evil inside her is responsible for these deaths. Only if she is aware of that—before it takes her over completely—will we have any hope of getting rid of this abomination."

Marnie stared at Hazel, nausea welling up inside her.

But Hazel wasn't finished. "You must act today, Marnie, because we can't afford to delay. Every day the demon will grow stronger. It has already killed many times and will do so again, so we have to stop it *now*."

Marnie switched her gaze from one to another. David looked as if he wanted to run away. Hazel's mouth was set firmly.

She couldn't avoid what she had to do.

"I'll go over there now," Marnie said reluctantly. "To Elinor's."

Hazel hoisted her bag onto her lap and produced a cheap ballpoint pen and a small notepad. She scribbled something down and tore off the sheet before passing it to Marnie across the table. Her cell phone number.

"Call me when you've seen her and tell me how you got on. I'm staying at the Four Winds Guesthouse on Lodge Lane. Do you know it?"

Marnie nodded. Four Winds was a cheap and cheerful B and B, a mile or so from where she lived.

Hazel pushed her chair back, narrowly missing a tall man in a pinstripe suit carrying a tray piled high with Big Macs, fries, and large Cokes. He swore.

"Sorry," Hazel said, clearly unconcerned, as the man went on his way, muttering.

David was also on his feet. "Bye," he said, looking scared.

Marnie was sure he would have given anything to have been tucked up in bed yesterday morning.

"Bye," she replied to his retreating back.

Marnie stood outside Elinor's front door. She knew how David felt. She wanted to run away too. What she needed to do was the last thing she would have wanted, but she must. Right now. Although *how* was a different matter.

She closed her eyes and pressed the bell. Within a few seconds, Elinor opened the door. "Hi, Marnie." Her face broke into a smile. "I'm really glad you're here. I've got some brilliant news." Marnie pasted a smile on her face and followed Elinor into her living room where she sat on the edge of one of the two matching armchairs. She didn't want to sink into the comforting depths of the settee. What if she had to stand up suddenly? Those soft, floral cushions were the devil to escape from once you had sunk into them.

Elinor threw herself onto the couch, her face radiant. "I've got an interview for that job I applied for as a bookkeeper. They rang me this morning and told me they want to see me next week. They sounded really keen too."

"That's wonderful news, Elinor. I'm so happy for you." Marnie hoped she sounded sincere. Knowing that in a few moments she would have to deliver some unwelcome news, she had to concentrate hard to keep her voice steady.

"Would you like a cup of coffee? Or a glass of wine maybe?"

Marnie shook her head. "No, I need to talk to you about something serious and I'm afraid you're not going to like what I'm going to say."

Elinor put up her hands defensively. "No. I'm not hearing any bad news. I'm only hearing good news today. Oh, did I tell you I had a dream about Steve? It started off as the house dream, only this time there was smoke coming out of the chimney, and when I opened the door, there he was, sitting in the chair waiting for me."

"Which night was that?"

"The night before last. The night you stayed over. Of course, I remember, I never got chance to tell you because you weren't feeling well."

"The night that woman was killed? The latest one?"

Elinor looked at her with a curious expression. "If you mean the suicide, yes, I believe so, but what's that got to do with anything?"

Marnie took a deep breath. "Because I—or at least we—think the two are linked. Your dreams and the killings."

Elinor blinked. "*What*? And who are 'we' exactly?"

Marnie took another deep breath. *OK. Here goes.* "The witness who saw the black cloud surrounding the last victim, and a woman who had experience of all this in Yorkshire ten years ago."

Elinor looked stunned. Incredulous.

Finally she spoke. "I can't believe you're sitting there, ruining the best day I have had for the past two years. I thought you were my best friend, Marnie. How could you do this to me?" She burst into tears.

Marnie jumped from her chair, went over, and tried to put her arm around Elinor, but she pulled away. Without warning, she turned and snarled, baring her teeth like a dog.

Marnie jerked away. "What the hell?"

Elinor glared. A faint trace of black smoke curled out of her nostrils. "Oh, my God. *Elinor.*"

The body was that of her friend, but the expression wasn't. The smoke was drifting out of the corners of her mouth. That was enough for Marnie. She grabbed her bag and ran out of the room, wrenched the front door open and fumbled for her car key. Slamming Elinor's door behind her, she pointed the key at her white Corsa and unlocked it.

Within seconds, she was driving away, breathing hard, her heart thumping.

She parked in her driveway and took out her cell.

Locating Hazel's number, she called her. Hazel answered almost immediately.

"Hazel? Thank God. I went round to Elinor's and, as you feared, whatever that thing is seems to have crossed over into her conscious mind. I started telling her about the link between her dreams and the deaths, and I hadn't even got very far before she suddenly turned on me. Like she was possessed by some demon."

She heard a deep sigh. "I'm sorry to have to tell you, Marnie, that she is."

"What? Possessed by a demon?"

"Yes. You must believe that what I told you this morning is true. Of that I have no doubt."

Marnie paused. What Hazel had told them at McDonald's was so far-fetched. "Surely that stuff is pure Hollywood."

Hazel sighed again. "No, Marnie, this demon is real and dangerous. You did right to get away, or you might have been its latest victim because, when that thing takes over, Elinor has no power to control what happens. It is the demon, not your friend, we have to deal with."

"Is that what happened to you? Did you become its victim?"

A pause, and Hazel said, "I think I'd better come over. It's too late tonight though. I'll come over tomorrow and explain everything."

Chapter Four

"Sometimes I wish I had never remembered what happened and that I still didn't know what a dream demon looks like or what it can do," Hazel said, as she handed Marnie a tissue to dry her eyes. Her heart went out to the woman who sat, crushed and huddling into the cushions of the brown leather sofa that crowded the cozy living room.

Marnie's anguished face seemed to plead with her. "Seeing Elinor like that. Like her body was there, but something evil had taken it over. I've got to help her, Hazel. You've got to tell me everything." A fresh wave of sobbing drenched the tissue.

Hazel handed her another, then another. She let Marnie weep, knowing the tears were necessary to let all the emotion out. If only she'd had a friend like Marnie when her Joe had been killed, but they had been the sort of couple who'd needed only each other. With him gone, she had been left truly alone. Eyes flooding, she looked down at her hands and let her gaze wander around the warm, welcoming room. Rather too much furniture left little floor space, but Hazel liked that. It felt familiar. Safe.

A generously upholstered chair had greeted her with a comforting sigh of softness as she had sunk into it. Rich red curtains swept the deep pile carpet with swirling patterns of gold, green and scarlet, colors Hazel herself would have chosen. In the traditional, tiled fireplace, a living flame gas fire gave off the illusion of blazing coals, adding to the warmth of the atmosphere, while above, the mantelpiece was crammed with framed photographs. Most were large enough and close enough to see their features. Marnie clearly came from a big family. So many faces were an echo of hers, with their unruly black curls and dancing eyes.

Not that Marnie's eyes were dancing now. Her heavy sigh snapped Hazel's attention back. Still cuddled into the sofa, Marnie emerged from behind the tissues, eyes bloodshot and watery. She blew her nose.

Hazel smiled. "Are you feeling any better, my dear?"

Marnie nodded. "A little. Thanks." She started to return the tissues and stopped. "I don't think you really want these back, do you?" A wry grin.

Hazel looked at the soggy mess. "Er—no, I don't think so."

They both managed a light laugh, edged with nerves.

Marnie took an audible, deep breath. "I need to know everything, Hazel. Please tell me. Help me understand what's happened to my friend and what we need to do to save her."

Hazel couldn't ignore this cry for help. Adrenalin pumped through her veins as she forced herself to recall the events of that terrible evening ten years earlier. She controlled herself with a few deep breaths, and started in.

"Joe was like the others. The demon had entered him, and he had desperately tried to get rid of it. I believe he was driven mad in the process. So mad that he honestly thought that if he clawed out his eyes, it would have to come out with them. But that's only part of its evil. As David told us, when he described the woman he saw, normally the cloud disappears entirely once it has entered the victim, but this time something else happened. I believe it must have killed Joe before it was fully absorbed and it left him—or at least a part of it did. When I noticed something like a black mist out of the corner of my eye, it attacked me. All I can remember is an unbearable pain in my left eye and ear and a feeling of utter despair, so bad I had to get rid of it. So I...." She stopped, reading Marnie's shocked expression.

"So that's when..." Marnie touched her own left eye.

Hazel nodded.

"But why did it let you go?"

Hazel shook her head. "To this day, I have no idea. For six months or more, I couldn't remember a thing and still, there are gaps. After it happened, I couldn't go back to that house. I never did. I sold it and moved to my little bungalow, cut myself off from everyone and everything I had known before and spent my life trying to understand what happened to Joe and me. There are still things I don't understand, including the main problem."

"What's that?"

Hazel sighed. "How to get rid of the bloody thing once and for all."

Marnie leaned forward in her chair. The tears were gone, replaced with fear. "But why Elinor? Why has this happened to her? And why now?"

Hazel shook her head. "I wish I had all the answers, but I don't. Legend tells us that the dream demon invades its host when a person is at their lowest ebb and controls their nightmares, transforming them into pleasant dreams by feeding on the negative energy of the nightmare. This energy is expelled from the victim as a sort of cloud, or pall, of stuff resembling black smoke. Some sort of metamorphosis transforms this into the demon itself, which goes in search of the first person it can find who is alone and, therefore, vulnerable. They don't even have to be asleep, or in any kind of trouble." Her heart pounded, the precursor of a palpitation. She laid her hand on her chest and took a long, cleansing breath.

Marnie was on her feet in a second. "Oh God, Hazel, are you all right?"

Hazel nodded, concentrating on keeping her breathing steady. Gradually the palpitations died down, and she grew calmer.

"Can I get you some water?"

Hazel shook her head. "No, I'll be fine in a second. I think there's a little too much adrenalin pumping through my veins." She attempted a smile. Unsuccessfully.

Marnie sat back down on the sofa.

Hazel knew she must continue. Marnie had a right to know everything. She clasped her hands tight for comfort. "Where were we?"

"What was it like—you know—when that— thing—attacked you? Do you mind me asking?"

Of course Marnie would want to know that, so she'd be prepared. Hazel's stomach churned. The thought of this innocent woman experiencing the horror…

She gulped down the bile and began, her words little more than a whisper. "I felt as if a vice had been clamped around my mouth and throat, and I tried to scream but nothing came out. Something was trying to force its way into me, through whatever entry it could find. My mouth, my nose, my ears. My eyes…"

Marnie's face was twisting in horror. She was hugging herself.

Hazel hesitated. Had she said enough? Maybe she had said too much.

A long pause. Hazel waited for some sign from Marnie that she was ready to hear more. Or that she had heard enough. The young woman was rocking back and forth like a distressed child.

The room was silent, save for the clock on top of a small corner table. Hazel was grateful for the rhythmic ticking. Normality and order in chaos.

Marnie stopped rocking. Hazel's stomach rolled again. She bit her lip and concentrated on keeping the bile down. When had she last eaten? Hours ago.

"I need to know anything else you can tell me, Hazel."

Oh no you don't, Hazel thought. *Not now and not ever if I have my way.* But she needed to show her one more thing. One important source of information that she would need to share and that they might be able to use soon. She leaned over and picked up her large bag from where she had placed it on the floor beside her chair. Marnie watched her.

Hazel took out a small, slim volume, ancient and bound in black snakeskin. Looking up, she read fascination in the younger woman's eyes. She tapped the book. "This is a bit of an oddity I found quite by chance on the Internet. It may answer some more of your questions. Not all, mind, but at least we know we're not the first to go through this. It's called *The Dream Demon*, and I've learned more about this entity through this little gem than from any other source." She turned over the fragile leaves carefully and began to read. "'The demon feeds on the terror of its victims. Through that it possesses their souls and returns them to hell from whence it came.'" She raised her eyes from the book. "I understand this to mean that in order to manifest itself, it needs a human who is going through hell to act as a host, and it goes off and feeds on the souls of others which it takes back to hell."

Marnie nodded slowly, as if trying to comprehend. After a pause, she spoke. "If it goes back to hell, surely it's left its primary human host. So why isn't Elinor free?

Hazel shook her head. "The author, Reverend Sargison, believes that the demon only releases a *part* of itself each time it goes off to feed on the souls of the innocent. All the while, most of it stays within the host, feeding off negative energy, regenerating and becoming more powerful all the time."

Marnie nodded again. "So, meanwhile, Elinor continues to feel better and better. But surely there will come a day when it has drained her of all her negative thoughts and fears. What happens then?"

Hazel shook her head. "That doesn't feature in this little book, I'm afraid. Evidently he didn't hang around long enough to see that happen."

Marnie frowned and looked down.

Hazel extricated herself from the chair and, with some difficulty, knelt in front of Marnie. She clasped Marnie's hands, but her tears were creeping back.

Hazel wanted to hug her and take away all the pain she knew she must be feeling. She resisted. They must both be strong. Too much work needed to be done.

For now, she settled for consoling words. "If it's any help, I do know how it feels to try and get your head around this. The thing I couldn't understand is, given there are so many people going through their own personal tortures, why aren't there more of these demons around? And why, therefore, aren't there scores more unexplained suicides? Finally I decided that this was the way it had been ordained. By the universe, or by God, call it what you will. Maybe there simply is only room for one dream demon at a time and maybe the choice of host is arbitrary. Who knows? Not me and not even the Reverend."

"What are we going to do about Elinor?" Marnie asked, tears making fresh rivulets down her cheeks.

Hazel had been dreading this moment since she'd arrived. She squeezed Marnie's hands tighter and inhaled. Best to get this over with. "The Reverend Sargison states that if the dream demon becomes aware of you, you're in trouble. If it is denied your soul the first time, it will try again. You told me that Elinor was awake during the manifestation today, and this means it's very strong within her." She took another deep breath. "Marnie, I'm sorry, but you mustn't see her again—at least not alone—until we can work out how to get rid of it."

Fresh tears poured down Marnie's face. She wrenched her hands from Hazel's grasp. "But she's my best friend. And she's in trouble. She *needs* me."

Hazel wanted to weep also, but she had to hold on for both their sakes. She kept her voice steady. "Yes, she does, but she needs you alive, not dead. You must see, Marnie, that if you are alone with her, the demon will sense your presence and will emanate from her as soon as she is upset in any way, whether she is awake or asleep. I wouldn't give ten seconds for your chances of getting out alive."

Marnie dabbed at her eyes with sodden tissues. "She's been so much better these past weeks. Since the so-called suicides began. She's even got a job interview in a few days. I never would have believed that a month ago."

Hazel nodded. She had heard all this before. "Reverend Sargison says that is because the demon is draining all the bad thoughts away, leaving a sense of increased well-being. Ironic, isn't it? In a dark and horrible way."

"So what happens to Elinor? If I can't see her, how can I ever help her?"

Hazel decided she'd better say the word and have done with it. "She needs an exorcism."

Marnie sat up bolt upright. "*What?*" Hazel struggled to her feet and stood over Marnie, who was looking at her as if she had stepped out of the looking glass.

"The Reverend performed a few of them—with mixed success if the account is accurate—but I believe we need to try."

Marnie stared at her. Hazel stared back, knowing she had to convince Marnie.

Finally, Marnie shook her head. "Do they even have exorcists these days? Or was that dreamed up by Hollywood?"

Inwardly, Hazel breathed a sigh of relief. She was getting through, and she hadn't had to tell Marnie the worst part either. "Oh, they do exist, but we would have to contact the church and persuade them that an exorcism was necessary, and I don't know what the reaction would be. I think the local bishop has to give his approval for anything like that, and the Church doesn't generally go around advertising who its official exorcists are."

Another lengthy pause. Marnie seemed to be battling with herself. Hazel hoped and prayed she had said enough.

Marnie stood and went over to the mantelpiece.

She selected a photograph and brought it back to Hazel, who saw a happy, beautiful young woman she guessed was Elinor, holding the hand of a laughing little girl with long, white-blonde hair. A beaming Marnie stood on the other side of her. Behind them were pine trees, and two red squirrels played nearby. Summer. A few short years ago. A world away.

"Coppice Wood. Red squirrel sanctuary. I remember that day so clearly. Just a few weeks before…" Marnie's voice tailed off.

Marnie had told Hazel what had happened to Elinor's family, but seeing the little girl brought everything into sharp focus. Tears in Hazel's eyes, she handed the photograph back. "She was a beautiful child." Her voice shook.

Marnie nodded and looked down at the picture, tears falling onto the glass. She wiped them off with her fingers, raised the frame up to her lips and kissed it. "For you, Laura. Rest in peace, my little angel." She carefully replaced the photograph on the mantel.

Marnie drew herself up, her shoulders shaking before going rigid. She turned around. The tears were gone.

She spoke and her voice was firm. Resolved. "Let's do it."

"Elinor, come to me."

She stood in the pristine kitchen of the little house she called Sanctuary. Outside, she knew was danger, but here inside, with a fire burning and crackling in the grate and her beloved husband standing, smiling, his arms outstretched to her, nothing could harm her. She reached out to him, her heart overflowing.

"Steve, it's been so long."

"I know, my love, but I'm here. I couldn't find you, but now I have. Come to me. You need never be frightened again. I promise. I'll protect you."

She hesitated, still not sure if this was the real Steve. This was a dream, after all. Dreams could turn nasty. She could look at him one second and see all the beauty and grace she remembered and in another moment, could be recoiling from a corpse, crawling with maggots and eaten by worms. Elinor shivered.

"What's wrong, my love?"

She shook her head. "Nothing. Just me being stupid." It had to be him. Elinor would hold back no longer. As she reached out her hand and their fingers touched…

Her eyes snapped open. For a second she expected to see a pine table and chairs, gingham curtains at the windows. And Steve.

"Damn!" She rubbed her eyes and pushed back the duvet. A pale daylight was trying to weave through the curtains. Still half-asleep, she peered out at a gray, wet world and yawned before closing the window.

Coffee and plenty of it. That's what she needed. Maybe a slice of toast as well. She patted her stomach. She'd been eating better, flesh was returning to her bones, and as she brushed her teeth and surveyed her reflection, she realized her cheekbones were no longer hollow. If she carried on like this, she'd soon look human.

She padded into the kitchen in her soft slippers and switched on the kettle, swiftly followed by the radio. The nine o'clock local news was on.

"Police are investigating the latest in a series of mysterious suicides in Hartshouse Wood. Late yesterday evening, they were called to Foresters Lane, scene of an earlier incident where a young woman died three days ago. The body of a man was found. He had apparently died of self-inflicted injuries. Police are appealing for anyone who may have seen or heard anything in the area to contact them immediately."

This is becoming an epidemic. Elinor switched to a music station and set about mopping her kitchen floor. Her cell phone rang. Marnie. "I thought I'd ring to see how you are?"

"I'm not bad at all. How are you?"

"Oh, I'm OK. But after the day before yesterday when... You know."

"Know what?" Her friend was talking in riddles. "When I came round and we were talking about the deaths."

"Oh yes. Terrible, isn't it? They said on the news that there's been another one, and it sounds as if *that* was pretty gory as well."

After a pause at the other end of the phone, Marnie sighed deeply. "You don't remember, do you?"

"I don't remember what?"

"I came round to talk about, well, the smoke, and you got upset and..."

Elinor was confused. What was this all about?

And why was Marnie calling her on a Friday morning? Shouldn't she be at work? "I'm sorry, but I don't know what you're talking about. What smoke? I don't remember talking about smoke. I haven't smoked for years and neither have you. Look, are you sure you're feeling all right? Do you want me to come over?"

"*No.*"

Elinor jumped at the vehement exclamation.

"I mean, no, that's fine, El. I'm fine. As long as you're OK. I have to go. See you. Bye." Marnie was gone.

Elinor clicked off her phone and carried on mopping the floor. But her thoughts were elsewhere and far from peaceful. What was wrong with Marnie?

Worse, Elinor had a sense that she was missing something important.

After returning home from work, Marnie set down her keys on the kitchen table and sighed, grateful for the early finish to a frustrating Monday. Her attention was caught by a half-full bottle of Chianti. She would normally wait until after dinner, but the wine was really calling to her. *If I have to put up with any more of Joy Farrell's tantrums, I swear I'll swing for her.*

Bad enough she had to go to work with everything else that was happening, but with no other income, she needed this job. And she had already taken three days off last week. The way things were going, she would probably need more time off too.

The Head wasn't pleased at the short notice, but what could Marnie do? She certainly couldn't reveal the truth. Sometimes she hardly believed it herself.

She took a glass out of the kitchen cupboard and uncorked the bottle, pouring herself a generous measure before taking her wine into the living room. She kicked off her black, low-heeled office shoes and settled down on the settee. Putting the wine on the glass-topped occasional table, she rubbed her cramped and aching toes, inwardly cursing the English teacher who had caused all the trouble today. Marnie'd been up and down those bloody stairs fifty times for the ungrateful bitch. Did she once say "thank you"? Did she, hell. Well, that would be the last time.

But even as Marnie thought it, she knew it wouldn't be. She was conscientious. She would say "yes" the next time and the time after that.

The doorbell rang. Oh God. What now?

She scurried on bare feet to answer it. "Elinor."

She was dressed in one of her old, but timeless designer dresses, accentuating her newly regained curves. Her makeup was immaculate and must have taken her ages to apply. On her feet, a pair of her once favorite black Jimmy Choos with impossibly high heels. Oh yes, the old Elinor was back.

Despite an instant of delight at her friend's apparent restored self-esteem, Marnie wanted to slam the door in Elinor's face. Hazel's warning and their last encounter had ensured that. But if what she'd said over the phone on Friday was true, she didn't remember a thing about what had happened. She would be horrified, and probably very angry, if Marnie did that.

And, with what Elinor had inside her, who knew what effect that would have? Maybe this demon could still get out. After all, smoke could seep under doors.

"Marnie? Aren't you going to let me in?" Marnie realized she was standing there, holding the door, her mouth slightly open. "I'm sorry. I've had a hell of a day. Joy was up to her old tricks again. Yes, come in, of course. Come in."

Elinor's gaze was weighted with curiosity.

Marnie shut the door, hoping and praying she was doing the right thing. She took calming breaths. She mustn't upset…it…that's all.

"Glass of Chianti?" Marnie asked, hoping her voice sounded normal.

"That'll be great, thank you."

Marnie brought another glass into the living room to find Elinor already on the settee. She poured some wine before retrieving her own glass and sitting on a nearby armchair. Elinor's look of surprise wasn't wasted on her, but Marnie couldn't bring herself to sit on the settee, having seen the evil lurking within. If only she could make Elinor understand, but Marnie was too scared to broach the subject today and prayed her friend wouldn't stay long.

And what could they talk about? How could Marnie tell Elinor that she and Hazel had spent the weekend contacting every church official they could find in order to get an appointment with an exorcist?

She took a swig of wine with a quivering hand, and her teeth clinked on the glass.

"Marnie, whatever's the matter? You're shaking."

Marnie thought quickly. "I'm all right. Just angry. That bloody Joy always manages to wind me up. I could throttle her sometimes."

"You've told me about her before. She sounds a real bitch." Elinor sat up straight. "Look, I'll tell you why I came round. I wanted to see you obviously, but I was worried about that phone call on Friday, because you didn't sound yourself at all. I couldn't get hold of you all weekend, and you seem really agitated today as well. Have I done something to upset you?"

Marnie nearly dropped her glass. "No, of course not. Work's getting on my nerves at the moment with all these prima donna teachers strutting around the place, bossing me around."

"Are you sure that's all?" she asked, sounding confused. "I mean, you seemed to be referring to something that supposedly happened between us when you came round the other day, but I can't remember anything wrong."

Marnie made a dismissive gesture with her free hand. "Oh, ignore me. Probably that time of the month or something."

Elinor's quizzical frown showed she wasn't satisfied with the explanation.

"Have you got a date for that interview yet?" Marnie asked.

Elinor looked bemused. "I'm sorry, I thought I told you. It's tomorrow at two. I'm a bit nervous about it actually. It's the first one I've had in years."

"You'll be fine. Be yourself." And Marnie prayed God they didn't upset her.

The phone rang, and Marnie had to restrain herself from leaping out of the chair to answer it. Anything to escape this awkwardness.

"Marnie? Hazel. Are you alone?"

"Elinor's with me." She hoped she sounded cheerful, given that Elinor was in the same room. Marnie swiveled round and smiled at her. Her friend returned the smile.

Marnie turned back, Hazel's voice urgent in her ear. "I was afraid of that. Try and get rid of her. I told you. It's dangerous for you to be alone with her."

Conscious of Elinor's eyes burning into her back, Marnie worked hard at keeping her voice light. "So where are you?"

"I'm getting out of my rental car outside Elinor's house. Remember, you told me where she lived the other day? I thought I would try to speak to her and carry on where you left off. When I realized she wasn't here, my first thought was that she had come round to see you. You must get her away, Marnie. The risks to you are too great if she stays there. I—oh, good grief!"

"What is it? What's happened?" Any pretense at keeping calm evaporated. Elinor couldn't have missed the hysteria that shot into her voice.

"Marnie?" Elinor called. "What's wrong?"

"Get her out, or you get out of there. *Now!*" The phone cut off.

"Marnie? Who was that? What's happened?" Elinor was beside her, one hand on her arm.

Marnie twitched, instinctive revulsion in every pore. She wanted to brush Elinor off, but was too scared to touch her. She forced herself to speak, her mouth dry. A lie formulated itself just in time. "Someone from work. Joy's been having a go at her too. Look, El, I'm sorry, but I'm going to have to go to her. She's really upset. Can we do this another time?"

"Of course we can. I'm sorry to hear that."

Marnie thought quickly. She would have to go to Elinor's house and see what had happened to Hazel. Normally she would give her friend a lift wherever she wanted to go, but she obviously couldn't this time.

"I'm really sorry, but would you be OK on the bus? She lives on the other side of town, and I've got to get there as soon as possible."

"No, no problem at all. I'll be fine. There's one every twenty minutes, and that's how I got here, after all." She laughed.

Marnie did her best to laugh with her, but Elinor's eyes were unusually bright. Glittery.

Despite the warmth of the central heating, Marnie shivered.

Elinor would watch from the bus stop, so Marnie reversed her Corsa out of her driveway and drove in the opposite direction, knowing she could go around the block and double back once she was out of sight. Once she was on the right road, her mind started to race. What could have caused Hazel to cry out like that?

A few minutes later, she turned into Elinor's road.

The empty, dark street was a little creepy. Marnie hurried, aware she had maybe fifteen minutes before Elinor's bus arrived. She parked next to the only other vehicle nearby, a dark blue Ford Ka, which must be Hazel's rental. Marnie went straight over and peered in. No one there.

She looked over at Elinor's front door, illuminated by a streetlamp framed by double windows with net curtains. One twitched. Hazel?

Fear prickled Marnie's backbone and raised the hairs of her neck. Yet, she could see no alternative. She would have to go up there. She had to find Hazel.

Her palms were sweating, and she was breathing hard, her heart racing. She crept to the front door and forced herself to look at the dark window. Nothing.

The net curtain stayed in place. But she had an overwhelming feeling of being watched.

Not bothering to try the door, which she knew Elinor always kept locked, Marnie raised her hand and pressed the doorbell, hearing its ringing echo in what should be an empty house. No reply.

She stepped back and looked up without seeing any lights on or any movement at either of the upstairs windows.

She went around to the side of the house, and opened the side gate to take her around to the back. Strange. Elinor usually kept that gate locked.

The small back garden was gloomy in the dark. Marnie tried the handle of the side door. Locked. She froze. She had heard nothing, but was certain that someone was behind her. "Hazel?"

Nothing. Yet she was still sure that someone was waiting for her to turn around. Maybe, any second, a hand would seize her shoulder. Or worse. But could anything be worse than that?

She squeezed her eyes shut, scared of what she would see, and spun around. Holding her breath, she opened them.

Nothing.

In the distance, she heard a car starting, the sound of its motor receding in the distance. Illuminated by the light shining through the neighbor's window, she caught sight of some ferns at the far end of the garden. They swayed a little.

Marnie shook herself, rubbed her arms and left, closing the gate behind her. She looked toward the road. Hazel's car was gone. It must have been the one she had heard starting. Somehow they had missed each other, although Marnie couldn't think how, as Elinor's garden possessed only one way in and out.

She glanced at her watch and quickened her step. Elinor's bus was due in five minutes. Just time to get to her car, drive off down the road and round the corner, off the bus route. Marnie unlocked her Corsa and got in, buckling her seatbelt with one hand as she started up the engine with the other. Something was bothering her. Something she couldn't quite grasp.

Until—

Those bloody ferns! They shouldn't have swayed in the breeze. There *was* no breeze.

Chapter Five

As soon as she rounded the corner, Marnie parked her car and got out her cell. She selected Hazel's number on the speed dial but got voicemail. "Hazel. It's Marnie. Please call me as soon as you get this message. I'm really worried about you."

She started the engine and drove back to the only place she could feel safe. Home. Her mind was everywhere but on the road.

Her cell rang almost as soon as she got inside. She grabbed it out of her bag. "Hazel. Oh, thank God. What happened?"

"I'm OK, Marnie. I've just pulled up outside your house. May I come in?"

"Of course. I'll open the door." She trotted to the door and jerked it open.

Hazel was pale. "I need a drink. Do you have a Scotch or something?"

"I'll get it. We'll go and sit down in the living room. Do you want water?"

"Just a splash please, dear."

"Ice?"

"Yes, please."

Marnie had the same, deciding that if Hazel needed one, pretty soon she would too, once the story was told. She waited until Hazel had taken a healthy gulp.

"That hits the spot. Thank goodness you had some in."

Marnie wasn't in the mood for pleasantries. She was far too wound up. "What's been happening, Hazel? I went over to Elinor's after we got cut off, and it was really weird there. I called your name, but you didn't answer and then you drove off."

"I was in the house."

"*What?*"

"For some reason, the front door was unlocked, so I walked in and, oh my God, what an atmosphere."

"Atmosphere? Sorry, I don't understand."

Hazel nodded, her hands stretched out in front of her, grasping her knees. "I felt it—thick and heavy, like pea soup. There's something in that house. Something evil."

"But I thought the demon was in Elinor." Hazel was wringing her hands, clearly uneasy.

"That's still the case, I'm sure of it, but there's something else. I don't know where it's come from, apart from hell, but it's there, in her house. The air was full of this—sort of—heaviness. Reverend Sargison had a similar experience." Hazel stopped.

Marnie realized she probably looked as horrified as she felt, but couldn't find words.

Hazel shook her head. "I'm sorry, Marnie. This must all seem very odd to you, and I can't really say much more. You had to be there. I had a feeling…a sense of pure evil and crushing despair."

Something else troubled Marnie, like a persistent itch. She hesitated, then decided she might as well ask anyway. So what if Hazel decided her imagination had gone into overdrive? "I don't understand how I could have missed you coming out of the house. Um, did you peek out of the net curtains?"

"Net curtains? No."

"And the ferns. They moved, and I thought it was the wind. But there *was* no wind."

"That was probably a cat or a bird."

Of course, Hazel had to be right about that one. In the darkness, Marnie could easily have missed a small animal. But as for the curtains… Imagination? Or something else?

She sighed. Her nerves were getting the better of her. Behind the dark glasses, Hazel was waiting, but behind that calm exterior, something was going on. Marnie felt a twinge in her gut. Hazel still had her secrets, but whatever they were, Marnie was too scared to ask. At least for now. So she settled for, "What do we do?"

Was that a slight smile at the corners of Hazel's mouth? "I think it's time we tried to get the church on our side."

Marnie nodded but wished she could stem the panic that was building up inside her.

The next day, Marnie watched the exchange between Hazel and the priest, her eyes darting from one to another. Like watching a tennis match where, any time now, someone would shout, "You cannot be serious!"

Father Thomas Walker was a middle-aged man of around fifty, with graying hair and a slight paunch.

He was also, as the Diocesan HQ had told Marnie, their designated exorcist. They hadn't actually used that term, but that was what she understood. She and Hazel had been at Church House for half an hour so far, but weren't making progress.

Of course, the Church must get hundreds of crank calls every year. If Father Walker took on every one of them, he'd never do anything else, and Marnie figured he also had a parish to run. She wondered if his parishioners knew about his other duties.

"Mrs. Messinger," he said, as if he was speaking to a recalcitrant child. "I didn't say the church wouldn't do it, I merely pointed out that we don't make a habit of performing exorcisms and we don't tend to advertise our services."

Hazel's already clear irritation bubbled to the surface. "Father, I don't think you understand the seriousness of this situation. People's lives are in danger. Eight, maybe more, have already died. This thing is out there, and it's on a killing spree."

The priest blinked rapidly. "If what you say is true, I can promise you I understand how dangerous it is."

"Oh, it's true all right."

The priest continued to sit, expressionless. "I assure you we will look into it and contact you in due course."

Hazel leaped to her feet. *"In due course?* Come on, Marnie, we're wasting our time here. It looks like we're on our own." She started toward the door.

Hazel's anger having infected her, Marnie needed no urging. She stood, ready to follow.

Father Walker also stood. "Mrs. Messinger, I must repeat. I didn't say we wouldn't help. I need to assure myself of the facts of this case. You must appreciate that the claims you have made are, at present, unsubstantiated, and I would have to look into the matter in a lot more detail before I could recommend to the bishop that we become involved. Please understand my position." He was placatory. Perhaps he feared a complaint to his bishop?

Hazel advanced closer to the priest. A little too close. He took a step backward. Marnie was dismayed. If he was intimidated by Hazel in a temper, what good was he going to be with a dream demon?

Hazel wasn't backing off. "I wish you'd appreciate ours. People are dead because of this demon, and more will most certainly die if someone doesn't stop it. So, will you help us or not?"

Despite their plight, Marnie felt sorry for the beleaguered priest. He looked at her, and his expression pleaded for help. Normally, she might have stepped in to cool the situation down. But these were not normal times.

Father Walker ran his tongue over his lips. "I cannot proceed until I have examined all the facts and—"

Hazel brushed him aside. "Right. That's it. We're out of here. Come on, Marnie." She strode to the door, Marnie behind her.

"Mrs. Messinger!"

Hazel turned back. "By the time you've examined all your precious facts, more people will have died. I hope you can live with that on your conscience, Father, because I'm damn certain I couldn't!"

Outside, Hazel was shaking, and Marnie put her hand on her arm. "Come on, there's a Starbucks over there." She pointed across the busy city street. "I'll buy you a cappuccino."

Hazel nodded and they were soon sitting with steaming mugs of frothy, fragrant coffee.

"Whatever would we do without caffeine?" Hazel smiled and examined her hands. "At least I've stopped shaking. At one point, I honestly thought I was going to throttle that man. His attitude reminded me of all the reasons I dropped out of the Anglican Church."

Marnie put down her mug and twirled the stirrer in the froth. "It still leaves us with the problem though. How are we going to get rid of this demon? However are we going to help Elinor when she doesn't even realize she's in trouble? And what caused you to feel as you did in her house yesterday?"

Hazel shook her head. "The answer to all your questions is that I don't know, but we do have someone on our side." She rummaged in her bag and pulled out the slim book. She turned the fragile pages with care and reverence. "Reverend Sargison recounts his encounters with the demon and how he performed the exorcism to get rid of it."

"I thought you said he had mixed success." Hazel paused and raised her eyes from the book.

"He did, but do you have any other ideas?" Marnie shook her head.

Hazel continued to leaf through the pages. She stopped. "Here we are." She scanned the page. "Have you got a notebook? I stupidly left mine at the B and B."

"I've got my diary." Marnie searched in her bag for a few seconds, found her pocket diary, and handed it to Hazel.

"That'll do, thanks." Hazel started to make a list. "We're going to need holy water. Are there any Catholic churches around here?"

"St Columba's up the road." Marnie stopped, shocked. "Oh Hazel, you're not going to steal holy water from a church!"

"I can hardly go to the supermarket and buy some, can I? We're going to need a small bottle to put it in. That at least we can get easily enough. Oh, and we'll also need a Bible and a couple of crucifixes."

"I've got a Bible at home. How big do the crucifixes have to be?"

Hazel scanned the pages. "He doesn't say, but I would guess they will need to be a reasonable size, and maybe we should wear them too."

Marnie caught the glint of Hazel's necklace. "Hang on a minute. What about your pentagram. Doesn't that help us at all?"

Hazel stroked it. She smiled. "Strange, isn't it? I seem to be reverting to my childhood programming. I won't take this off though, just in case."

Marnie smiled too. "Always hedge your bets."

Hazel winced and dropped her hand from the necklace.

"What is it? What's the matter?" Marnie reached for Hazel's hand.

Hazel got there first, covering it with her other one, but not quite quickly enough, for Marnie saw something wriggle under Hazel's skin. She rubbed her hand before hiding it under the table.

Marnie's fear trebled, squirming in her stomach, growing into a twisting, corkscrewing panic.

Something was seriously wrong with Hazel. Something she hadn't explained. "Hazel. What was that? What did I just see?"

Hazel stopped massaging her hand and brought both of them into view. "What was what?"

Marnie pointed at the hand, which now seemed perfectly normal. "I saw something move under your skin."

"Oh, that was a muscle spasm. I get them occasionally. Don't worry, it's nothing. I'm fine now."

Marnie continued to stare at Hazel's hand. She was lying, but why?

Hazel drained her mug. "Come on. There's no time to lose. We've got work to do."

Marnie stood, leaving half of her cappuccino, but taking new questions along. Who was Hazel, really? Marnie was entrusting herself and her best friend's well-being to a virtual stranger.

Marnie knew little about the woman except that Hazel lived in a small bungalow in Yorkshire. Ten years ago, she had had an encounter with a dream demon and survived.

All of this had come from the woman herself. How could Marnie be sure any of it was true? And assuming it was, and Hazel had been spared, why hadn't the demon finished her off as it had all the others? She was scarred, of course. Blind in one eye and deaf in one ear. Had she done that to herself, as the others had? Or had something, or someone, done it to her?

What had Marnie seen crawling under Hazel's skin? It had been such a brief glimpse, but it looked like a wriggling worm. Or maybe not wriggling. More like *rippling*. Like a tiny wave.

Marnie had far more questions than answers, but in their current circumstances, what could she do?

Elinor was in mortal danger, and the only person who appeared to have a clue about what was happening to her was Hazel. And the mysterious Reverend Sargison, of course.

The city streets were teeming with traffic as they emerged from Starbucks. Horns blared. Buses rounded corners and followed each other in convoys. Hordes of people inched their way along overcrowded streets. Marnie followed Hazel, whose eccentric appearance in Gothic black and purple raised not one eyebrow.

They stopped at a pharmacy, where Hazel bought a small plastic bottle with a screw top. "Perfect," she said.

They came to a jeweler's where Marnie's credit card secured them two small silver crucifixes on chains. "We really could do with a larger one but I expect these will do," Hazel said.

Marnie hoped so. Her credit card didn't leave much leeway for any more sizeable purchases. When they got to Marnie's car, she asked, "Where do you want to go, Hazel? Back to my place?"

Hazel shook her head. "I think we'll go to the church first and on to your house to fetch your Bible. Then we'll go to Elinor's."

Marnie nearly dropped the ignition key. "*Elinor's*? Are we ready for that? Surely we need to rehearse. Or at least decide what we're going to do. How we're going to broach the subject with her."

"No. If we're doing this ourselves, we need to do it now. That demon's already very strong and growing all the time. You didn't feel what I felt in her house."

Marnie hesitated. The knot of fear crept further up her gullet. Any higher and it would choke her. A solid ball of terror filled her throat, threatening her air supply.

She started the engine and backed out of the parking space in the multistory car park. "God, Hazel. I hope you know what you're doing."

Hazel sucked in an audible breath. "So do I, Marnie, so do I."

The old church was silent but open, much to Marnie's surprise. "I thought they locked all city center churches these days to stop vandals."

"Thank goodness they didn't lock this one." Hazel located the holy water font and unscrewed her bottle, ready to fill it.

"Hang on, Hazel," Marnie whispered furiously. "Maybe it's open because the priest's here. Maybe he's hearing confession or something."

The two women listened, but all Marnie could hear was her own breathing, ragged and nervous. She looked around at the tall stone pillars, the vaulted timbered ceiling and down the aisle, past the rows of ancient pews, to the stained glass east window, and the impressive altar.

Hazel filled the bottle, and its metal top scraped as she screwed it back on. The sound rasped across Marnie's already shredded nerves.

"I'm done," Hazel whispered, the sound echoing around them. "I don't suppose they could spare one of those." She pointed at one of the large brass crosses in a small chapel to their right.

"*Hazel!*" Stealing from a church!

"All right. It was just an idea." She sounded annoyed. Surely she couldn't have been serious.

Oh, she was. Marnie was sure. That was part of the problem. And why so much about this business didn't quite add up. She knew so little about Hazel…

After picking up Marnie's Bible at her home, they parked outside Elinor's house. "This is a good time, I guess," Marnie told Hazel. "El should be at her job interview."

Hazel checked again. "Are you sure she said two p.m.?" Her hands trembled.

"Yes. Are you sure you want to go through with this? Don't you want us to plan it all a bit more first?"

"No. We need to get inside that house before she gets back and this time, we need to be more thorough. Last time, I allowed myself to be frightened off, but now I've got you with me, I shan't be so easily deterred."

Fear crept up Marnie's spine, and she shivered. "I wouldn't count on me being any good. I'd give anything to drive off and forget I ever knew anything about this."

Hazel nodded, then winced, as if a sudden pain had attacked her. "I feel the same. Fate does cruel things to us sometimes." She was clasping her hands, which rippled again. The waves seemed to be stronger and more pronounced.

"Another muscle spasm?" Marnie asked, watching for Hazel's reaction.

"Yes. I think I need to see the doctor when I get back home."

Why wouldn't Hazel trust her? This time Marnie couldn't stop herself. "You're lying to me. But I don't know why."

"I hope to God you never find out either." She sounded frightened and tired. "Come on, we have work to do."

Marnie stared after her as Hazel opened the passenger door and scrambled out. The unanswered questions would have to wait. Pressing the key fob to lock the car, Marnie looked down the road at the small, semidetached houses. Like little boxes. Each with its pocket handkerchief lawn and neat flower borders. In the front windows of some homes, early Christmas trees glittered, waiting to be lit.

Plastic snowmen and reindeer littered the gardens.

All was quiet and peaceful. Marnie guessed most of the residents were at work, and the children were at school. Who would ever believe that such middle England respectability could hide an evil force that was killing the local inhabitants?

Marnie shivered and turned her attention to Elinor's house. Net curtains at all the windows to keep out prying eyes. But what were they keeping in?

Hazel tried the front door. Locked this time. They rounded the house to the small side gate. She unlatched it, with Marnie surprised to find it unlocked. The old Elinor would never have left her doors or gate open. She followed Hazel through to the back garden. They stuck to the narrow pathway that led around the side and back of the house. Marnie noted the clump of ferns. They were still, as they should be on a fine, chilly day with a weak sun trying to brighten the world. No breeze stirred the air, and no animals rustled the leaves.

"Right, let's see if there's a way in here." Hazel tried the side door, but, as expected, this too was locked.

"There's the conservatory round the back," Marnie said. "But surely Elinor hasn't left that door open."

She hadn't, but she'd neglected to lock one of the windows securely, and with some wiggling and persuasion, it eventually opened. Marnie decided she must tell Elinor to get the locks fixed on these windows. Anyone could break in.

She stopped short. So what was she doing, if not breaking in? If anyone saw them, surely they would call the police? She looked around. The area was visible from only one house, and Marnie couldn't detect any motion in the one overlooking window.

"I don't think I can squeeze in there, but you could." Hazel had already located a small bench and dragged it into position for Marnie to climb up on.

She did so, reluctantly. "I'm really not sure about this, Hazel. I mean, if anyone saw us they'd think we were nothing better than burglars."

"We haven't got time to worry about that. Come on."

Was Hazel angry? Or was Marnie's fear speaking? Fear, smothered in trepidation. She scrambled onto the bench. Level with the sill, she shoved the window open wider. She squirmed inside and hoisted herself over the window frame. A bit of a squeeze, but she made it. She dropped down onto the floor and rushed for the conservatory door, some distance from her entry window. While the bolts slid back easily enough, the mortise lock on the door was secured.

She went back to the open window. "Hazel. I've got a problem. The door's locked and there's no key. I'm going to have to look for it."

"Damn! Do you know where she might keep it?"

Marnie shrugged her shoulders. "I haven't a clue." A few nondescript potted plants caught her attention on the windowsills. She checked underneath each but found nothing, so she returned to the window.

"Could she have taken it with her?" Hazel asked.

"She could, but I've never known her to use this door to get in. There would be no need. No, I reckon she would have left it here somewhere. But it could be anywhere. Is there no way you could squeeze through this window?"

Hazel pointed at herself. "What do you think? You had a job getting in and you must be at least three dress sizes smaller than me."

Marnie looked around for any larger windows but they were all the same. "I'm sure Elinor keeps a spare front door key in the kitchen. In one of the drawers. I'll go and check." She scurried into the hall.

And stopped, halted by the chill.

What was that? A faint, whooshing sound. Where from? Her palms were sweating. Her breath came in short, shallow pants. She couldn't delay. She must find that key. To the left of her was the living room and to the right, past the stairs, the kitchen.

Straight ahead was the front door. Maybe she would be in luck, and Elinor would have only locked the Yale. She hurried down the short hall and tried it. No chance. Locked with the mortise, just as she'd guessed.

Marnie turned back to see something creeping down the stairs, black and amorphous, serpentine in its movements.

She froze, horrified. Heard a scream. Hers.

She rushed into the kitchen and at the side door saw another mortise lock, with no key.

The thing on the stairs must be closing in on her. She wouldn't be able to get past it to the conservatory. Pray God Elinor kept all her spare keys together.

Marnie frantically rummaged through drawers filled with tablecloths and tea towels, heedless as they spilled onto the floor. Hearing the swishing sound draw near, she fumbled through the cutlery drawer. On one side of the cutlery tray lay a bunch of three similar keys, all for mortise locks. "Lucky," she murmured. The side door was closest. She could open that and call to Hazel from there.

But by then, Hazel was banging on that door. Yelling something Marnie couldn't make out. Behind her, the whooshing sound was almost on her.

She dashed to the door and jammed key after key into the lock with shaking fingers. The third key worked, and Marnie turned the handle, wrenched it open and was met with a white-faced Hazel on the doorstep. But she wasn't looking at Marnie.

By the angle of her head, Hazel was looking into the house. "Marnie, get out here. And whatever you do, don't turn round."

Chapter Six

Elinor waited. She glanced at her watch. 2:15. They'd kept her waiting twenty-five minutes. She couldn't blame them for the first ten, because she'd been early. But if you make an appointment for a certain time, you should be there. That's how she had been brought up anyway. Punctuality was important. It showed respect for the other person. Tardiness on the other hand... Elinor's annoyance was building.

Just because they held the power to give or deny her the job didn't mean they had the right to be rude.

With great difficulty, she swallowed her anger and was surprised to find a strange, unpleasant taste in her mouth. God, she couldn't afford to have bad breath. She opened her bag and found a small box of Tic Tacs, flipped it open, and popped a couple into her mouth. The sharp spearmint flavor dissipated the foul taste almost instantly, and she calmed herself again.

By 2:30, she was on the point of asking the bored secretary how much longer she was going to be kept waiting. A door to the side of her opened.

A tall, smartly suited man greeted her. "Mrs. Gentry? I'm Malcolm Lake, Managing Director. I'm sorry to have kept you waiting. I had to take an urgent transatlantic phone call, I'm afraid. Would you like to come in?"

He showed her into his office. She took in the large executive chair, all black leather and chrome. Expensive. The light oak desk, equally large and impressive. A laptop stood open at one side of it, while an iPad lay directly in front of where he now sat. He indicated the much smaller chair on the opposite side of his desk and smiled at Elinor, showing brilliant, white teeth.

No one had teeth that perfect except with considerable professional help. This guy was minted. Elinor, resentful, found the unpleasant taste flooding her mouth again. She hoped he wouldn't be able to smell her breath. With any luck, she was far enough away. And she was seated at a lower level than he.

"Mrs. Gentry. Elinor." Again that expensively enhanced smile.

Elinor forced herself to smile back at him.

"Your application form is very impressive. I see that you are a certified accountant, so why would you want to be a lowly bookkeeper for us?"

"I don't see it like that," she said, straining to keep the annoyance out of her voice. "I enjoyed my career as an accountant, but I see this position as one I could really enjoy and enhance with my experience. I feel I would be able to bring not only highly developed bookkeeping skills but also add value through my accountancy knowledge."

He was nodding at her like a bobble head doll. "That's a very good answer, Elinor." Why did he sound as if he didn't believe her? "But if we take you on, won't you use us as a springboard to the next accountancy job that comes along?"

The bastard. So what if she did? What the hell business was it of his anyway? At least he'd have had the benefit of her knowledge and experience.

She was fighting even harder to control her emotions, and the foul taste was becoming stronger with every second. "I applied for this job because this is the job I want. I love bookkeeping. There are other aspects of accountancy that I don't enjoy, and that is why I didn't apply for an accountancy position, nor do I have any intention of doing so."

Malcolm Lake leaned back in his chair, her application in his hand. He studied her face for a few moments before glancing back down again. "It says here that you left your last position two years ago.

What have you been doing since then to keep yourself motivated?"

Elinor took a deep breath. The question she had most feared had been asked. "A few months before my job ended, I lost my husband and daughter in a road accident, so I took some time out for myself to deal with my grief."

"Two years is quite a long time. Do you feel you're quite over it now?"

She stared at him. Over it? How could she ever get over losing her husband and only child? Who was he? A man or a monster?

She gagged on the saliva filling her mouth, then coughed into her hand. Once, twice… She couldn't stop. *Oh God, I'll never get this job.*

She looked over at him. Lake's face had blanched paper-white. He sank back in his chair and raised his hand, pointing at her.

She was drifting, drifting away on the cloud of smoke in front of her eyes. Everything was fading. Slipping away. She could hear herself coughing, as if far in the distance. The room was shrinking. *She* was shrinking. The smoke was everywhere. She could hear agonized screams. First a man's. Then a woman's.

Then blackness.

———

Marnie did as Hazel told her and ran out of the house. Hazel shoved past, into the house, and slammed the door shut behind her.

Marnie heard the sound of the key turning and tried the handle. Locked. She banged on the door. "Hazel. What's going on? Let me in!"

"Stay out there, Marnie. Don't try to get in. Whatever you do."

Marnie heard another noise. A rushing sound accompanied by a ferocious snarling and a baying that sounded as if it came from the depths of hell itself. The racket would surely have brought the neighbors running out if any of them had been around. She banged on the door again, terrified. "Hazel! Are you all right? *Hazel!*"

As suddenly as it had begun, the commotion from inside stopped. Marnie heard the key being turned in the lock. She waited. The handle didn't turn. She pressed her ear against the door.

Nothing.

Her right hand trembled as she opened the door a tiny crack. She listened again. Still no sound from the other side. She called, "Hazel?" No reply.

Frightened at what she would find, she opened the door wider.

The kitchen was a mess. Coffee had been spilled everywhere, mixed with sugar and eggs and the contents of the drawers she had turned out in her frantic search for keys. Some dinner plates lay smashed on the floor, but no sign of Hazel.

Marnie paused on the threshold, listening for any sound, but the house was silent. Hardly daring to go any farther, she struggled to push her fears aside as she took first one step and another. Out of the kitchen and into the hall.

She crossed into the living room and snapped on the light. Everything was neat and tidy. No evidence of any struggle in here, and still no sign of Hazel. She checked the conservatory. The window stood open, just as she had left it. She heard a sound behind her and turned. In a corner of the room, something dark shifted.

"Hazel, is that you?" Grasping the remains of her courage, Marnie crept toward the corner. Hazel was lying, apparently unconscious, on the floor.

"My God! Are you OK?" Marnie felt for a pulse.

Racing.

Hazel stirred. "Marnie?"

"Thank God. Can you move? Can you stand up, do you think?"

Hazel struggled to sit up and instantly put her hands to her head. "I have such a terrible headache. It's pounding."

"Here, let me help you. We have to get out of here. Elinor is bound to be back soon. She mustn't find us." Marnie helped Hazel to her feet and half- carried her out through the side door, without caring that she had left it unlocked and the conservatory window wide open. What if burglars did get in?

Whatever was unleashed in that house would soon put paid to their plans.

Struggling under Hazel's weight, Marnie was glad she'd parked nearby. She unlocked the car and helped Hazel into the passenger seat, then checked the time. 3:05. She would drive out of Elinor's road and round the corner, park and see to Hazel, who was moaning a little and seemed to be only half-conscious. Maybe she should go to the hospital?

Hazel was cradling her head, leaving her hands and arms partially revealed. The rippling effect had intensified so that small waves appeared to be rolling under her skin. There. Again. But this time, much worse. What was causing that? Who *was* this woman? *What* was she? Marnie's head was pounding, and the nausea was almost overwhelming.

Marnie struggled to keep her composure. "Hazel. Can you hear me?"

She was still moaning. She had to have been in agony.

"Hazel? It's Marnie. I'm trying to help you. Shall I get you to a hospital?" Screwing up her face, she reached out her hand, swallowing hard at the revolting rippling. She tugged at Hazel's right arm and managed to pry it away from her head. Her left hand slowly dropped at the same time.

"Hazel. Look at me."

The moaning stopped. Hazel turned her head slightly. Her large dark glasses fell into her lap and, for the first time, the full effect of the terrible scarring to the left side of her face was revealed. It looked as if an animal, perhaps a large cat, had gouged great scratches from her forehead, through her eye and onto her cheek.

Marnie's mouth filled with bile. She clapped her hand over it, closed her eyes, and gulped down the sour stuff. When she dared to move her hand away, her voice croaked. "Hazel."

Hazel opened her eyes, two pools of black liquid. Marnie screamed.

―――――――

"Marnie! *Marnie*."

The voice floated into her consciousness from far away, along with a furious knocking. Marnie opened her eyes, taking a moment to realize where she was. In the driver's seat of her car, seatbelt unfastened. She must have passed out.

And she was alone. Where was Hazel?

Elinor was banging on the window, looking frightened. Her smart navy interview suit was stained, although what with, Marnie couldn't register in her befuddled state. Elinor's hair was untidy too.

At that moment, she looked a world away from the chic designer-clad woman who had knocked on Marnie's door the day before.

"Are you all right? What happened?" Elinor opened the car door and helped Marnie out. "You look terrible. What happened to you? Why are you here?"

Why *was* she here? For a second, Marnie couldn't remember, and then everything flooded back. Hazel. Those terrible eyes. The *thing* in Elinor's house.

What about the thing in Elinor herself? And where the hell was Hazel?

Marnie clutched her head. "I don't know. I'm not sure..."

"You'd better come inside."

"*No!*"

From Elinor's shocked expression, Marnie knew she sounded hysterical. Desperately, she struggled to clear her mind and focus on appearing normal. "I'm sorry. I...I need to get home. I'll call you tomorrow."

Elinor continued to stare. "I can't let you go like this. Marnie, you look dreadful. What on earth has happened? I'm back from my interview and I saw your car—"

"Did you see anyone else? An older woman, dressed like a hippie?"

"What? No."

"Have you been in your house yet?"

"No, I've only just got back."

But she seemed unsure, even panicky. Marnie's mind raced. Whatever was in Elinor's house shouldn't attack her because, in so far as anything about this mess made sense, the thing had emanated in some way from Elinor herself. It would hardly attack its host—or creator—or whatever she was.

Marnie, on the other hand, was in great danger both from the thing in the house and from her friend. If only she could explain! But bearing in mind what had happened last time, explanation was not an option.

Certainly not now. She had to find Hazel. But those eyes...

Marnie wrenched open the car door and clambered back into the driver's seat.

Elinor watched. "Marnie, I don't understand what's going on." She sounded lost, confused.

Despite Marnie's fear, the tug of their old friendship pulled at her. A part of her wanted so much to give Elinor a hug, but she was too scared. Marnie shut and locked the car door.

Elinor knocked on the window. Her voice was muffled and her expression nervous. "Marnie, I think I need help. I think something awful happened this afternoon, but I don't know what."

Marnie started the engine and fastened her seatbelt. "I'll call you. I promise. I'm so sorry, but I have to go."

As she drove off, she caught sight of Elinor's face in the rearview mirror. Alone and frightened. Tears filled Marnie's eyes, and she blinked them away.

She glanced at the clock on the dashboard. 3:30. She couldn't have been unconscious for more than a few minutes. Hazel must have needed some of that time to recover herself. The woman with the frightening eyes had been in no fit state to go anywhere unaided. Logic dictated that she couldn't have gone far.

Sure enough, a little way down the road, Hazel was standing at a bus stop, her large, dark glasses back in place. Marnie stopped the car, and Hazel hurried toward it as fast as her lack of fitness and plus-size frame would allow.

Not ready to be in a confined space with her, Marnie unsnapped her seatbelt and scrambled out of the car. "Hazel, what the hell happened? Your eyes— "

Hazel, a little breathless, raised her hand. "I know, Marnie, and you deserve an explanation. Can we go somewhere? Is there a café around here where we could have a quiet chat? I appreciate you won't want me in your house yet, until you feel you can trust me again. I haven't been completely honest with you, and that's wrong of me, but I intend to put that right this afternoon if you'll let me."

Marnie hesitated. Hazel sounded her usual self, but was she? Logically though, Marnie couldn't do much else. Right now, Hazel was all Marnie had. At least she might find out what Hazel had been hiding.

Marnie's nervous stomach gave yet another lurch at the thought. What was this secret Hazel had tried to keep?

Marnie took a deep breath. "I think there's a little place around the corner from here. You'd better get in."

Hazel smiled. "Thank you. I promise everything will make more sense when I explain."

"I hope so. I really do. I don't think I can go on like this much longer. It's scaring the hell out of me."

They both got back into the car, and Marnie started the engine, still unsure she was doing the right thing. They drove in silence until they came to a small row of businesses containing a neat little coffee shop.

"This will do," Marnie said and, five minutes later, they were sitting with cups of coffee. A dozen people were spread out among a handful of tables covered in clean, white cloths, and they were chattering enough so she and Hazel wouldn't be overheard. But Hazel, sitting opposite, spoke so quietly that Marnie had to lean forward to hear her.

"It's difficult to know where to start, but I suppose the best place is with the book."

"Joshua Sargison's book?"

Hazel nodded. "First of all, I haven't told you that my maiden name was Sargison. The Reverend Joshua Sargison was my great-great grandfather."

Marnie hadn't seen this coming. "Bloody hell!"

Hazel smiled. "That was my reaction when I found out. He was born in 1820 and died in 1875 and I don't know anything about him as a person other than those dry, basic facts." Her voice dropped to a whisper. "Everything I've told you since we first met is true, but what I haven't told you is that, when I got this book and read of a similar encounter Joshua had experienced and survived, memories started to come back. They were awful, black memories of the attack itself." Her voice cracked and she paused to sip her coffee.

Marnie's gut-wrenching anxiety gave itself another turn of its tortuous rack. She pushed her rapidly cooling coffee aside. Nothing would have stayed down anyway.

Hazel lifted her glasses and wiped her eyes. "When I got home that afternoon, Joe was sprawled out on the lawn. I thought he'd had a stroke or a heart attack or something and I raced over to him. When I got there, I turned him over and… His eyes were staring at me, his mouth was open, and he looked as if whatever he had seen had terrified him to death. Except it hadn't. It had made him—"

"You don't need to say anymore. I can guess," Marnie said, as gently as she could manage while her heart pounded a tattoo in her chest. "Like the others, you mean?"

Hazel nodded. "Also, what you don't know is, when it attacked me—it left something inside me."

Marnie recoiled. Her eyes darted around the now bustling café. Laughter mingled with the clink of coffee cups and tinkle of cutlery. Tables and tables of normality. If only they knew… All she could think of was how she could escape. She turned back to Hazel, who wore a wry smile.

Fear turned to disbelief. Marnie also had the thought that if Hazel wouldn't always wear those bloody glasses, maybe a person could divine what was going on in the woman's mind.

"Don't worry, Marnie. I won't harm you."

"Doesn't this make you the same as Elinor?"

Marnie managed at last.

She shook her head. "No. I'm the opposite of Elinor. I'm the antithesis if you like. Sort of matter and antimatter, so we're polar opposites."

"I don't understand. The demon entered you. You tried to claw your eye out to get rid of it. You must have felt all the negative emotions the others felt."

"I did, but I believe it was the same demon Reverend Sargison encountered. It didn't kill him and, for some reason, didn't kill me and I think those reasons are one and the same. Perhaps it's because we're related. Here, I'll read you the passage where he talks about it." She searched in her bag before brandishing the book. She hurriedly flicked through the pages until she found what she was looking for.

"'I confronted the devil that poured from Miss Norton's mouth. It was truly foul and despicable and I pronounced it be gone. But it charged at me, and I was momentarily overwhelmed. The demon entered me, and my spirit was flooded with such despair that I must surely expire. I fell to the floor, clutching at my throat and was sore troubled. I prayed to the Lord for deliverance, but still the demon raged within me. On and on it swelled, smothering my very being, trying to deny my faith, my very Christianity. I was in the depths of despair, deafened, my face a bloody mess, my left eye already gone and the right one on its way. And all by my own hand.

"And then, with the last vestiges of my sight, I saw a bright light. It warmed my body and soothed my soul. Soon the light entered me and I felt it surround the demon, encasing it in a prison of gold, deep within me. Then my ordeal ended and I must rest.

"The demon shall no more trouble me for it is imprisoned in chains that will not break and walls that cannot crumble. My Lord God has delivered me from evil to walk in His light forever."

Hazel shut the book. "And that is the end of his story."

Marnie sighed. "Did you see a bright light?"

Hazel nodded. "In my case, it must have happened much faster because I didn't do as much damage to myself as Joshua did. At least I kept the hearing in my right ear and the only physical scars I have are here." She touched her left cheek.

"But did you have the sensation of the light encasing the demon? Like Joshua described?"

"Not quite as intense, but I do know the demon's still inside me. And it's trying to escape."

Marnie had a sudden realization. "Is that the—sort-of—wave I have seen crawling under your skin? Is that what made your eyes go black in the car?" She shuddered.

Hazel sighed. "Yes. I'm afraid it is. Oh, you're quite safe from me. I'm as certain as I can be of that, but I don't really know what to do about it. It all started when I got here, and I'm sure it's because of the demon that's possessing Elinor. They're two of a kind, you see. I've only really worked this out in the last few days, and I'm sure we ought to be able to use this to our advantage. I saw the demon behind you when we were at Elinor's house. It could have taken you at any time, but it seemed to hang back. When I confronted it, it eventually backed off. I think it must have sensed a similar presence in me, and that made it behave differently. Maybe that's a clue as to how we can get rid of it."

"Perhaps it thought I was your prey and it couldn't take me."

"Honor among demons, you mean?" Hazel's laugh was hollow and mirthless.

"I'm worried about Elinor. She had that interview today, and I never asked her how she got on. She looked so forlorn when I left, but I couldn't stay. I couldn't even tell her why."

Hazel squeezed Marnie's hand. "We'll think of something, my dear, and get your friend back."

Marnie squeezed back. "I hope so, Hazel. I really do. It's awful that she has been so much happier and on top of things recently, and it's all been a sham. Bought at the expense of other people's lives."

Hazel sat back and said nothing. Her silence was deafening.

"Is there something else?" Marnie asked. "Something you haven't told me?"

"I don't know, and that's the truth. I wish I did. I think the best thing we can do is go back home, or in my case, the B and B. Let's try and get a good night's sleep and maybe our subconscious will work out the missing bits of the jigsaw."

Back home that evening, Marnie fixed herself some tomato soup and a cheese sandwich while going over everything in her mind. None of it made much sense. All of it would sound crazy to anyone not directly involved.

Presently, she picked up her phone and checked.

No voice messages. She switched on the TV news, hoping for a distraction, and sat in her living room, remote in hand.

"Police are today trying to trace the whereabouts of a woman, said to be in her thirties, seen leaving the premises of a financial services company, between two thirty and three p.m. this afternoon. She is wanted for questioning in connection with the murders of Managing Director Malcolm Lake and his secretary, Marianne Johnston. Missing from the office is Miss Johnston's laptop which is believed to have contained Mr. Lake's appointment diary."

Marnie sprang to her feet.

The CCTV footage they showed was grainy and featured someone who could have been any one of a number of women. But Marnie was sure the tape showed Elinor, laptop under her arm, racing out of the main entrance and into the street. The fleeting glimpse was damning. The police wouldn't take long to identify her.

But when Marnie had seen Elinor, there had been no trace of the laptop. What had she done with it?

Maybe she had left it in her car, in the trunk most likely. Out of sight and maybe forgotten. She'd probably have no memory of what happened.

Or maybe she did. Perhaps that was why she had seemed so lost when Marnie had left.

The phone rang. She picked it up.

"Marnie? It's Hazel. Have you seen the news?"

"Yes."

"That *was* her, wasn't it?"

"Yes." Marnie's voice was a whisper.

Hazel sighed deeply. "We're going to have to act quickly and we daren't leave it later than tomorrow. I'll have to work out what we need to do."

"Maybe you should convert back to Christianity."

After a pause, Hazel said, "I already have."

Elinor didn't know how long she had wandered the streets near her home after Marnie had driven off. She had hoped to clear the fog in her brain, but still nothing made sense.

She was shivering as she picked her way up her drive in the darkness. Once inside, she flicked the light on and dropped her keys on the hall table.

Her breath choked in her throat. Something was wrong. With mounting panic, she dashed to the kitchen. Why was the light on in there?

Staggering slightly, she took in the mess in the kitchen and the open side door. Burglars. Great. What next? Elinor ran from the kitchen into the conservatory and saw the open window. She hurried into the living room, where another light was on, though nothing else was out of place.

There were so many blanks. Too many. Elinor put her hand to her head and thumped it hard. What was going on here? Why could she remember so little about this afternoon? Had she really been to the interview? Who had done this to her house?

Oh God, what if they were still here? She stopped and listened, not daring to breathe.

The house was still. Silent. They had gone.

She took the stairs by twos, finding every door open. She advanced toward her bedroom.

All the lights went out, leaving her in utter darkness. The door slammed shut in front of her. Elinor screamed, tried the handle but it wouldn't wiggle. She stumbled to the bathroom door. It banged shut in her face.

Scared to the point of hysteria, she turned to face the spare bedroom. She'd taken two paces before that door closed also.

"Elinor, Elinor."

The familiar, masculine voice sounded, as if from far away.

"I'm down here, Elinor. Come down the stairs. I'm waiting for you."

"Steve? Is that you?"

"I'm waiting for you, Elinor. Won't you come down to me?"

"Oh, Steve, I'm so scared."

"There's no need to be scared, I'll take care of you. Come down the stairs."

Elinor stood at the top of the stairs and looked down. The staircase seemed longer, so long she couldn't see to the bottom. The light. She needed to switch on the light. Fumbling for it, she flicked the switch, but nothing happened.

"I'll guide you, Elinor. You don't need the light. I am your light."

Elinor gripped the handrail, which was oddly rough to her touch. That a polished wooden banister was rough made no sense, but what did that matter? She was going to see Steve. He was waiting for her at the foot of the stairs.

She started her descent. Below her, the stairs seemed to wind. She lost count of the number of steps, which also made no sense. The staircase had exactly thirteen steps, but she'd gone down at least twenty. Still the calm voice called to her, a little closer as she descended farther and farther.

She looked to the side into darkness. Something more that made no sense. There should have been a white wall on her right and the banister on her left, but she sensed nothing except darkness and emptiness.

Out of the corner of her eye, she could have sworn something scurried away. She caught her breath.

But that wasn't possible. None of this was possible. She was in her home. And she wasn't dreaming.

Still she descended. Deeper and deeper. Hurrying toward the voice that urged her on with gentle persuasion.

"Just a few more steps, Elinor. You're nearly there." The voice was much closer. Soon she would be in Steve's arms.

She put out her right foot. And missed the step.

It had vanished.

She was falling. "Steve! Help me!"

Elinor opened her eyes. She was lying face down on the carpet. Her hall carpet. Even in the dark, she could see enough to make out its familiar pattern.

How much time had passed? She hauled her torso upright, wincing. Her legs were sore, bruised no doubt. She looked upward at her staircase and remembered missing her footing, although how many stairs she had fallen down was a mystery, especially when she'd descended so many.

Steve.

Tears sprang to her eyes. Had it really been him?

Or some cruel hallucination? Yes, it had to be that. Steve was dead. It couldn't have been him.

She wanted to get up and managed to extend an arm. She reached for the banister.

And touched flesh. Cold. Deathly cold. And dry.

She hardly dared to breathe. She couldn't bear to look.

"Elinor. Don't be afraid, I'm here. If you look up, you'll see me."

"Steve." Her voice was a shaky whisper.

"I'm here, my darling, and Laura's here. We're all together again. There's nothing to fear."

She looked into the face of her dear, dead husband, let him caress her, and pretended his cold flesh was the warm embrace she hadn't felt for more than two years. She closed her eyes and leaned against his chest while he stroked her hair and rained soft kisses on her cheek.

Kisses of ice.

"Come with me, my love. Come."

"Where are we going?"

"Home."

"But this is our home."

"Not anymore, we have a new home."

He was leading her farther down the ever-darkening hall. She could barely see him, though he was only inches away from her. This was wrong. This couldn't be happening. He couldn't be here.

A swirl of black smoke enveloped her and he was gone… If he'd been there at all.

She screamed, *"No!"*

The smoke billowed and swirled around her.

She stood, hands clenched at her side. "This isn't real! It isn't happening."

But still it billowed, and she heard voices all around her. Nasty, vicious, biting little voices. But the smoke didn't enter her. It didn't even choke her.

It disappeared.

The meager light filtering through the door returned. She was standing by the cupboard under the stairs. With relief, she realized she could hide inside and wait until morning, when everything would seem better. Maybe some of the strangeness would begin to make sense. And in the morning, she could call Marnie. Marnie would help.

Elinor bent, unlatched the door and crawled into the cramped space. She couldn't stand, but the closeness and the darkness were comforting, like a hibernating bear's cozy cave.

She heard voices. One was familiar. Marnie.

Thank God.

She fumbled for the latch, then remembered the door couldn't be opened from the inside. The joiner had never envisaged anyone needing to get out.

"I'm in here," she called as she banged on the door, hoping they would hear her.

The door opened.

Marnie woke in the middle of the night, thirsty. She pushed the duvet aside and made her way into the bathroom, running cold water into her tooth mug and drinking it down in one go. In the bathroom mirror, over the sink, she caught sight of the dark circles under her eyes that bore witness to her exhaustion. Despair overwhelmed her in a tidal wave of crushing sorrow. She lowered the glass onto the sink, letting the tears of anguish fall. How much more could she take?

But she couldn't turn back. Elinor depended on her. Needed her. And in a strange way she didn't fully understand, so did Hazel.

Still sobbing, she slid down onto the bathroom floor and for the first time since childhood, clasped her hands in prayer. "Let this be over soon," she begged God. "Please."

Finally, the tears subsided and she dragged herself to her feet, clinging to the sink to steady herself.

She had just climbed back into bed when the phone rang. She looked at the clock. 1:10 a.m. Peculiar time to be calling anyone. She picked up the receiver.

The voice on the other end was muffled, indistinct. "Marnie, it's Elinor. Please come, I'm scared. I think something's trying to kill me."

Every instinct Marnie possessed told her to hang up and pull the phone out of its socket. But she couldn't do it. They had been friends for too long.

Whatever was possessing Elinor had to be destroyed, and Marnie would do everything she could. She couldn't ignore her friend's cry for help.

"I'll be there as soon as I can. And I'll bring help." She called Hazel. A sleep-laden voice answered. "Hazel, Elinor called. She's in real trouble. She thinks something is trying to kill her, and she's asked me to go round there. She sounded really scared. Can I pick you up on the way?"

After a pause, Hazel said, "I'm not sure this is the right thing to do. The demon won't hurt her because it's *her* demon, and maybe it's a trap. It knows you, and it wants to lure you to it. I told you they were devious. I'll bet it's using Elinor to get to you."

"But she needs me, Hazel." Marnie sobbed. "I can't simply abandon her. Look, if you won't come, I'll have to go on my own."

"You will do no such thing!" Hazel's sigh was exasperated. "Oh, very well, pick me up. And may God protect us."

"I certainly hope so." Marnie ended the call, then dressed quickly in jeans and a warm sweater before picking up her bag. She grabbed the small crucifix she'd draped over the bedside lamp. She left her house, car keys in hand, one arm in and one arm out of her coat.

The winter night was freezing. Frost glittered on the windscreen, but a terrified Marnie wouldn't let the weather slow her down. She took a can of deicer from the trunk and sprayed it liberally all over. She didn't wait to scrape it off.

The road was quiet, with that heavy, leaden atmosphere peculiar to the winter months. Marnie drove as fast as she dared on the slippery road, with her windshield wipers at double speed, scattering bits of melting ice and deicer left and right, while the fan was at full throttle to clear the condensation.

Hazel was waiting outside her B and B, wrapped in a warm woolen coat and long red scarf. Shivering, she climbed into the car.

"Have you had any further thoughts about how we're going to do this?" Marnie asked.

Hazel buckled her seat belt. "Some, but it depends on what we find when we get there. If Elinor really is afraid, it must mean that she knows something. Maybe she's remembering, or has seen the demon for herself, or maybe she's just suspicious."

Marnie drove off. "She sounded scared stiff on the phone. She seemed to be talking through her hands or through a scarf or something. Her voice was muffled."

"Really?" Hazel seemed particularly interested. "Did it sound as if it was coming from a long way off? As if she was holding the receiver at some distance?"

"Possibly. Yes. That would be one explanation. Why? Do you think that's significant?"

"It might be. Are you quite sure it was Elinor?"

"Definitely. I'd recognize her voice anywhere." She shot Hazel a quick glance before returning her attention to the road. "You know something, don't you? Something about that call. Something you're not telling me."

"I don't want to say until I'm more certain. For now, let's prepare ourselves for whatever we're going to find there because if I'm right, we're going to need all our energy for that."

Marnie glanced over again. "You're as scared as I am, aren't you?"

Hazel sighed. "There's no point in denying it. Yes, I am. I've been scared stiff ever since I started remembering everything. I didn't tell you how that happened, did I? How I got my memories back." She took a deep breath. "It started as a dream with disconnected bits of information that made no sense, until one day, reading a passage from the book, I suddenly had a flashback and over the next few days, I had a series of them. Each one was more terrifying than the last. Finally, came the worst vision of all. I stared the dream demon in the face. That's if you can call it a face. I had visions of tormented souls, weeping and swirling in agony. Its eyes are those of a monster, consumed with hate, and its mouth is an infested, stinking chasm. Black… endless…insatiable."

Hazel stopped for a moment, as if she couldn't bear to carry on. But then she continued, "You can't believe the hold it exerted and the battle that raged inside me. I felt I was slipping deeper and deeper into it and screaming for help. Out of nowhere, a strong hand seemed to pull me back and I survived, although I don't know how. But the price I paid was to live with the dreadful knowledge that one day I would have to face it again. That day has come."

Chapter Seven

A t 1:45 a.m., Hazel and Marnie parked outside Elinor's house. No lights were on. Frost had turned the sidewalk white, and it glittered in the light from the street lamp as they made their way up her drive.

Marnie rang the bell and pushed slightly at the front door. Open. She exchanged apprehensive glances with Hazel, who urged her on. Marnie took a deep breath and shoved the door wider. She reached around and flicked the light switch, but nothing happened. She repeated the action a few times. Still nothing.

"Elinor?" Marnie called. "It's Marnie. I'm here, and I've brought someone with me. We've come to help you. Where are you?"

She heard a shuffling and banging, like someone knocking on a door. A familiar but muffled voice said, "I'm in here."

"It's coming from the stairs," Hazel said. "Does she have a cupboard or something?"

Marnie remembered. "Yes. Around here somewhere." She started feeling for the latch and found it. It turned and opened. Someone slowly crawled out backward.

"Elinor. Oh thank God." Marnie helped Elinor to her feet and hugged her shaking body, forgetting all about everything except that she was safe. For now at least.

A shivering Elinor was still dressed in her navy suit, both stained and badly creased. Her pantyhose were ripped, and she had lost her shoes somewhere. Her hair was lank and unkempt. She was shivering. With fear, Marnie guessed, rather than cold. "I was so scared, Marnie. You won't believe what's been going on here tonight."

"This is Hazel." Marnie waved at Hazel, who gave no more than a thin smile. "It's so dark," Marnie continued. "What's happened to the lights?"

"I don't know," Elinor said. "But it's probably lighter in the conservatory."

They stumbled there, and the chill hit them.

Moonlight illuminated the still open window. Hazel went over and closed it tight. She was back in an instant, and her trembling was visible even in the ghostly silver light.

"It's here, isn't it?" Marnie asked.

"What's here?" Elinor asked, her eyes wide and frightened.

"The thing that's been causing all the deaths in Hartshouse Wood," Marnie replied. She took a deep breath. "And most recently, the murder of Malcolm Lake and his secretary this afternoon."

Elinor gave a cry and stepped back. "*No!*"

Hazel was clasping her hands together tightly, and Marnie knew that if there had been more light, she would have seen that rippling along her arms.

"I think you know now, don't you, Elinor?" Hazel's voice was calm. "Where is it, my dear?"

"Where's what?" Elinor sounded wary.

"That young woman's laptop. The one you took from her office so they wouldn't know it was you who came to see Malcolm Lake this afternoon. Where did you put it?"

During the lengthy pause, Marnie could hear Elinor's breath coming in gasps. She herself was freezing, her hands almost numb with cold.

"In my car," Elinor said brokenly. "I swear I've only just realized. Oh, my God, Marnie, what have I done? What's happening to me?" She burst into tears.

Marnie reached over to hug Elinor, only to be stopped by Hazel's words.

"No, she has work to do. We both do, don't we, Elinor? That's why you called Marnie tonight, isn't it? You knew you needed help to defeat it."

Elinor's brows drew together. "I don't remember calling Marnie, although I'm glad she's here."

"No. You have no conscious control over this because that thing inside you is eating away at your soul and your humanity. But somewhere, deep in your mind, something clung on. I believe you managed to transmit your thoughts to Marnie, using the telephone as a medium because your friendship has been so strong for so long. I thank God for it. It gives us a chance."

Elinor seemed distressed, out of it, as if in some kind of trance. Marnie edged closer.

"Step away from her, Marnie," Hazel snapped, her voice harsh and dictatorial. "This isn't a request. If you don't do as I say, I will have to push you away and you really don't want me to do that. Not in my current condition." She took off her glasses.

Elinor screamed and collapsed. "You're not real!"

Marnie recoiled from the sight of the black liquid pools that were Hazel's eyes. They glinted and shone with pale, golden shards of light, piercing the shadowy gloom of the conservatory. Scared as she was, Marnie couldn't break free from their mesmerizing hold. They seemed to overwhelm everything in that room. And they pulsed with light. Ever changing, growing, and…possessing. They seemed to be reaching into her soul.

Unable to tear her gaze away, but desperate to do so, she started to feel her way backward across the room. She stopped, sensing something—or someone—behind her.

Elinor was crouching on the ground, sobbing and hugging herself, as though trying to make herself smaller. She kept repeating the same words over and over. "No, you're not real. You're not real."

"So *you're* here." Hazel's harsh voice chilled Marnie. "I wondered if you would come, and now it is time."

Marnie found she could look away from those terrible eyes. Turning, she peered into the gloom to see a shadowy figure standing motionless a few feet away. He had shoulder-length white hair, a stern demeanor, and black, or very dark, clothing of an earlier era. His gaze was fixed on Hazel.

"Who is that?" Marnie asked.

"Haven't you guessed yet? This is my great-great grandfather, the Reverend Joshua Sargison, only Elinor doesn't see him. She sees someone else, don't you?"

Elinor momentarily stopped sobbing and looked up. "Steve." The sobbing started again and intensified so she was keening, rocking back and forth. And despite the danger, Marnie desperately wanted to hold her, hug her, comfort her. But she remembered Hazel's warning to stay back.

"Reverend Sargison has returned to help us. All of us. Haven't you?"

The answering voice was gentle, but firm. "Yes, my child. We have much work to do before sunrise."

"Marnie," Hazel said, "you are to stay away from us. Whatever happens, you must not interfere and you mustn't touch any of us or come any closer than you are now. Do you understand?"

"Yes, Hazel." Marnie shrank still farther away, close to the wall.

"Reverend Sargison, let us begin. I have holy water."

"The demon within her is too strong for that. Stronger than those before it. This time, there can be only one outcome."

"Nevertheless, it must be done. Too many innocent souls have perished."

"The devil is greedy for innocent souls."

"He shall have no more through her."

"Then it is settled."

Hazel and the Reverend linked hands over the still sobbing Elinor, moonlight shining on the strange trio. They started chanting and circled around her, whirling ever faster until Marnie became dizzy. Their chanting became louder and, in the far corner of the room, a silvery light flickered and brightened. Like a candle, but the flame was larger. Whiter. It shimmered and floated toward the figures in the center of the room.

Marnie stayed where she was. Even if she had wanted to, she doubted if she could have moved.

Elinor had stopped sobbing and crouched on all fours, snarling, doglike. Through the legs of the couple who encircled her, Marnie saw her...*its*... eyes, red and gold, raging fires, the fires of hell.

"Oh God!" she exclaimed.

The hellish eyes stared at her. They seemed to cloud over. No. They weren't clouding over. Dark smoke was issuing from them. Coming toward her.

Marnie screamed.

The eyes pierced through the smoke, pulsing with fiery light. Chanting reverberated around her. Some from the Reverend and Hazel. Some from far away. An evil, stabbing rant. Marnie clapped her hands to her ears, but she could still hear it. Beating and rhythmical. Drawing her in against her will.

Above Elinor, a shadowy, smoky face was forming, only partially concealed by Hazel and the Reverend as they circled, their hands still interlocked above Elinor's crouching, metamorphosing form.

The face opened its mouth. The gaping black maw grew wider until it overwhelmed Elinor's body. Within it, writhing shapes snaked and entwined, like tongues. Marnie couldn't see Elinor any more.

She was gone.

The demon's foul breath hit Marnie, and she screamed, slammed by waves of hate and despair. She slid down the wall until she huddled on the tiled floor, hands clasping her knees, her face streaked with hysterical tears.

In a few seconds, the demon would surely escape and take her as it had so many others. Its presence was so strong she could feel it, so strong she could almost touch it.

She raised her right hand in a claw, ready to strike at herself. Any moment now, the smoke would reach her and invade her body.

It mustn't get in. She must stop it. Its closeness was oppressive. Inches away. Creeping. Insidious. Ready to send her to hell.

Her hand was poised, long nails aimed to rake at her eyes, pain overwhelming her.

"*No, no!*" she screamed repeatedly. She couldn't stop herself. Her nails were ready to do their terrible job. "*Please God, help me.*"

A powerful voice rang out. "In the name of God the Father—"

Joshua Sargison was interrupted by the demon's roar. Marnie's hand froze. The Reverend raised his voice above the din, as the white light closed in on the circling figures and their satanic prisoner. He continued, "God the Son and God the Holy Spirit, I bid you be gone, foul demon. Be gone to the fires of hell!"

The white light closed in. Growing, taking form, stretching out ghostly tendrils that encircled the group like comforting arms. The demon smoke withdrew a little, and Marnie's horror lessened.

Her hand dropped. She sobbed and shivered as the demon dissolved into a tower of smoke that receded into the space between the Reverend and Hazel, who stopped their circling. Still, they chanted while the demon howled and bayed like an animal in pain as, again and again, its attempts to escape were thwarted by the shimmering, morphing light.

Shapes emerged and receded from the imprisoning glow, swirling, golden figures with halos. *Is this what angels look like*? A wave of calm flowed over Marnie, dissolving her fears.

Bathed in the light, Hazel and the Reverend were still holding hands. Her eyes were closed, and she was smiling. Her skin had taken on a silvery glow.

The Reverend's face was turned away, but Marnie could see he was dressed in a Victorian parson's black suit and hat.

The roar of the demon faded to nothing. In the center of the circle, the smoke cleared. Elinor was returning, gaining substance, and becoming real again.

Becoming herself again.

"Oh God, thank you!" Marnie resisted the temptation to rush to Elinor, waiting for Hazel's signal that she could do so. After all that had happened, Marnie wasn't about to disobey the woman who had saved their lives.

Gradually, the silver light dimmed. As it faded, the Reverend also faded.

Two standing figures remained.

The lights came on. Hazel gasped and opened her eyes. No longer black pools. Marnie blinked rapidly and struggled to her feet. Elinor burst into tears.

"Is it over?" Marnie asked, wiping her tear streaked face with the backs of her hands. She'd nearly attacked herself with those hands. She shuddered.

Hazel nodded, rubbing her chest. Continuing to pant for air, she seemed to be having trouble breathing. "The demon has gone from Elinor. We have sent it back to hell where it belongs. There will be no more killings after tonight."

"Can I go to her?"

"Yes, you must. She'll need you. You only have a few minutes."

A new fear clutched at Marnie's heart. "Why?"

"Because she and I only have a few minutes. The demon was very strong." Hazel's breath was coming in labored gasps, and her face was gray. "It is…the…final…price."

Marnie felt like a scared little girl. "I don't understand."

Hazel smiled through her obvious pain. "The light will be coming back for us and it will take our souls away. I will return to Joe, and Elinor will be with her Steve and Laura. We will find peace at last." A smile began to form on her lips.

Elinor swayed as though she was about to faint. "Oh my God!" Marnie rushed over to catch Elinor.

Hazel sank onto a wicker chair and clutched her chest, gasping for breath.

"Hazel!"

"Stay with Elinor, Marnie. I'm ready. She's not." A final gasp and a rattling came from Hazel, dying away as Marnie held Elinor in her arms. Hazel was beyond help, but Elinor? Could she be saved? If Marnie phoned for an ambulance, maybe one would arrive in time.

But if Elinor lived, what would she face? The police would be sure to trace her before long, and she would probably spend the rest of her days in prison. Or a mental institution. Was that any way for her life to end?

"Oh, Elinor. I wouldn't have had this happen to you for all the world."

Her eyelids flickered and opened. "Marnie?"

"Yes, I'm here." Tears poured down her cheeks.

"There was something inside me, but it's gone now. I feel…empty."

Marnie bit her lip. "Not long, Elinor. And you'll see Steve again."

"I thought that was him today, but it tricked me."

"It's done." Marnie rocked Elinor like a baby. "You're safe."

Elinor's eyes closed, and her breathing became shallow. Marnie let her tears fall unchecked as she cradled her.

Elinor's eyes opened again, and Marnie's old friend smiled up at her. "You're such a wonderful friend, Marnie. The best. Thank you, but I'm ready. There's a wonderful light. Steve's there and Laura, and it's really them, this time. I know it…" She slumped.

"Elinor? *Elinor.*" She touched Elinor's neck but couldn't find a pulse. After all they had been through, after everything they'd done, it had not been enough. Her best friend was gone. But her soul was safe.

Marnie held her close and sobbed. "Rest in peace, Elinor. My friend." Through swollen, damp eyes, she gazed at the woman slumped dead on the chair.

"Rest in peace, Hazel. Thank you. Without you…" Marnie stopped. Words seemed inadequate.

Shouts and bangs preceded three uniformed policemen bursting into the conservatory. One of them pointed at Elinor. "That's her."

"We've got her," another one called to someone behind him.

"Would you mind stepping away from the suspect, please, madam," the third one said to Marnie.

Marnie laid Elinor gently on the floor and closed her eyes with tender care. She stood and did as she was told. Instantly they descended on Elinor. Like crows, she thought, feeling sick.

A fourth figure appeared in the doorway. He was dressed in a heavy, dark blue overcoat over a white shirt and navy tie. Even through her grief and crowded emotions, she registered that he was one of the best-looking men she had ever seen. He held out an identity card. "DCI Lucas. Tom Lucas," he added, smiling at her.

"She's dead, sir," one of the officers said, as he stepped away from Elinor.

"So is this one," the second policeman said, as he checked Hazel for a pulse.

DCI Lucas eyed Marnie. Questions lurked in his brown eyes. "Miss?"

"Redman. Marnie Redman." She struggled to control the quiver in her voice. "These are my friends. Elinor Gentry and Hazel Messinger. I can't explain everything, but they both died a short while ago. I think they had heart attacks, but I'm not sure."

"That's a bit of a coincidence, isn't it?" The second policeman sounded cynical.

DCI Lucas glared at him. "I'm quite sure Miss Redman will tell us what she knows down at the station, won't you, Miss Redman?"

Marnie nodded. She was beginning to realize how damning this must all look for her. If only Hazel could have hung on long enough, she could have explained it all far better than Marnie could.

"There are signs of a struggle of some kind in the kitchen." The voice arrived before the policeman did.

"Perhaps Miss Redman could explain that too," DCI Lucas said.

"I'll explain whatever I can. But whether you'll believe me—"

"All you need to do is tell the truth. We'll take it from there." He smiled again, and Marnie felt the beginnings of a tentative hope. If anyone was going to believe her, Tom Lucas would. Although, for the life of her, she had no idea how she could be so certain of that.

"I'll take her in my car," he said. "Sergeant Stewart, you're driving."

"Yes, sir," the cynical policeman replied. "If you would come with me please, Miss Redman."

Marnie nodded, turning for one last regretful look at Elinor and Hazel. The uprising of grief inside her would have to wait until after she had tried to explain a series of impossible events to an unimaginative police force.

DCI Lucas caught her eye and gave her a reassuring smile, again raising a tiny pang of hope. Maybe it would be all right after all. Sergeant Stewart led them out and she followed, with DCI Lucas behind her, while his colleagues secured the house.

The dawn was cold and pinkish-gray. A few birds were stirring. Thick frost crunched as Marnie stepped on it. She pulled her coat closer around her to keep out the chill, and her breath formed clouds around her. She experienced a strange sense of detachment, as if she hadn't really gone through the events of the previous few hours.

Behind her, Tom Lucas also drew his coat closer around him, and clasped his right hand with his left. His eyes grew darker, and a smile twitched his lips.

Under his skin, something rippled and squirmed.

About the Author

Following a varied career in sales, advertising and career guidance, Catherine Cavendish is now the full-time author of a number of paranormal, ghostly and Gothic horror novels and novellas.

Her novels include: *The Stones of Landane, Those Who Dwell in Mordenhyrst Hall, The After-Death of Caroline Rand, Nemesis of the Gods trilogy: Wrath of the Ancients, Waking the Ancients,* and *Damned by the Ancients, Dark Observation, In Darkness, Shadows Breathe, The Garden of Bewitchment. The Haunting of Henderson Close, The Devil's Serenade, The Pendle Curse* and *Saving Grace Devine.*

The Crow Witch and Other Conjurings is a collection of her previously published and brand new short stories.

Her novellas include: *The Darkest Veil, Linden Manor, Cold Revenge, Miss Abigail's Room, The Demons of Cambian Street, Dark Avenging Angel, The Devil Inside Her,* and *The Second Wife.*

She lives by the sea in Southport, England with her long-suffering husband, and a black cat called Serafina who has never forgotten that her species used to be worshipped in ancient Egypt. She sees no reason why that practice should not continue.

You can connect with Cat here:

Website: catherinecavendish.com/
Facebook: facebook.com/CatherineCavendishWriter
X (formerly Twitter): twitter.com/Cat_Cavendish
Instagram: instagram.com/catcavendish/
Tik Tok: catcavendish
Bluesky @catcavendish.bsky.social

Curious about other Crossroad Press books? Stop by our website:
http://crossroadpress.com
We offer quality writing
in digital, audio, and print formats.

Subscribe to our newsletter on the website homepage and receive a
free eBook.

www.ingramcontent.com/pod-product-compliance
Lightning Source LLC
Chambersburg PA
CBHW022044170626
46808CB00003B/1357